The Realm of Tiny Giants

Books by Dale E. Lehman

Howard County Mysteries

The Fibonacci Murders
True Death
Ice on the Bay
A Day for Bones

Bernard and Melody Capers

Weasel Words
Rooftop Sonata

Science Fiction

Space Operatic
The Belt
Penitence

Short Story Collections

The Realm of Tiny Giants
Found by the Road
Manifest Secrets

THE REALM

of

TINY GIANTS

stories by

DALE E. LEHMAN

RED TALES

Chase, Maryland

Published by Red Tales, 2021
Baltimore, Maryland
United States of America
https://www.DaleELehman.com

Trade paperback: 978-1-940135-98-4
Ebook: 978-1-940135-99-1

Dedication

For Jocelyn, who kept things running and made sure we didn't forget too much during difficult times.

No AI tools were used in the crafting of these stories. Seriously, where would be the fun in *that*?

THE STORIES

Introduction

Through my teenage and early adult years, I wrote a truckload of short stories. I cut my writing teeth on them, although in hindsight pretty much everything I penned back then was pretty awful. But the first steps of a toddler always are. We cheer baby steps not for their precision but their audacity and promise.

The stories in this collection came decades later, after a long dry spell followed by several novels. When I returned to short stories, I began small with flash fiction, compact tales of less than a thousand words. "The Lighthouse" came first, written as an entry for a weekly flash fiction contest with an almost brutal length limit—two hundred fifty words—hosted by the website Indies Unlimited (IU). To my surprise and delight, it won the Editor's Choice award for that week.

I became a regular entrant in that contest, contributing stories most every week over the following year. My pace did slow—today I contribute only sporadically—but by then I had won several awards and assembled an extensive collection of tiny tales. In this volume, you'll find a number of them, including four IU Editor's Choice winners and two honorable mentions.

Success came in other forms, too. "An Incident at the Mall," a flash tale written as a joke, introduced Bernard and Melody Earls, the stars of my novel *Weasel Words*. These infectious husband-and-wife thieves went on to appear in half a dozen short stories before the novel appeared. The first four of them are reprinted here. And *Weasel Words* itself? It just won Diabolic Shrimp's Golden Shrimpy Award, which may sound like a joke, too, but is real.

Longer tales soon followed, appearing in online publications hosted by Medium.com, most notably *Lit Up*. A number of these stories are reprinted here. Although none of them won awards, many are among my favorites, and two achieved a special measure of distinction. "Hurricane," written for a *Lit Up* contest, made the cut for the short list during the selection process, while the longest piece in this collection, "The Gift of Empathy," was selected for a *Lit Up* anthology forthcoming probably in 2021, although as of this writing no publication date has been announced.

A few of these stories have even led double lives, appearing first as flash fiction and then in longer form, sometimes radically altered. "The Stones on the Shore" made that transformation well before *The Realm of Tiny Giants* was conceived, while "The Crossing" was expanded specifically for this collection.

That, in brief, is the story behind these stories, save one important detail. Whatever their origin, in the preparation of this collection every one of them benefited from the attention of my wife and editor, Kathleen. It has been so since we met forty-five years ago. But for her helping hand, my literary baby steps might never have attained whatever maturity they now possess.

Running Down the Track

(Selected by Lit Up as a "star" for 2018)

His ears overflowing with clacking and creaking, Al Zullo had fallen asleep in his coach car seat as the train rushed headlong into twilight on its way from Denver to Chicago. Five cars ahead, the train's horn quietly screamed at every crossing, a comforting, beckoning wail. He may have dreamed, although he couldn't say. He seldom remembered his dreams, and when he did they had no clarity, rather like his life. "Always running," his mother had once said. "From what? You don't remember. To what? You don't know, or maybe even care."

Mother had always been right, for all the good it did her. Or him, for that matter. She was gone, and he was still running.

In the wee hours under a darkened sky, the train lurched and threw Al against the window. He woke with a start, those words echoing in his brain: *you don't even care.* They slapped his face and boxed his ears and washed his mouth out with soap. He sputtered, then wiped his lips with his sleeve. Eyes wide with alarm, he looked left where, beyond the window, night still reigned; then right where a young woman, a redhead, slept on in spite of the jostling, her seat reclined full back, her footrest up, her unshod feet delicately perched on its edge, a navy blue coat draped over her body. Al knew the woman's name, or had the previous day. She introduced herself when she took her seat, said she was going home from college for spring break, but now he'd forgotten all but that. His mind always had been a sieve, except where numbers were concerned.

College. Al had left his college days far behind. *More's the pity,* he thought. If he weren't so old, she might have taken an interest in him. Yes, she might've. He'd been an athlete once, after all. Track. Baseball. Held his school's record for bases stolen. The traffic accident that messed up his left leg ended all that, but he'd kept himself active. She wouldn't have noticed that bum leg. Not in bed, anyway.

He realized too late that they weren't alone. Another passenger shuffling down the aisle had stopped beside them, a dark skinned-fellow not much his junior. The man grinned down at him, and when Al looked up in embarrassment the other pointed at the woman and made a thumbs up gesture. Then he motioned Al to follow and moved on down the aisle toward the lounge car.

Al watched him for a moment, wondering who he was. He looked familiar, like maybe the father of someone he had once known, but, as with the woman, he couldn't put a name to the face. The man stopped at the door and turned. *Come on, man*, he mouthed, then grinned at the still-sleeping woman.

Good thing she is *sleeping*, Al mused, *or we'd both be thrown off this train.*

The other man passed through the door, which banged shut behind him. Al rose, steadied himself on the headrest of the seat in front of him, and gingerly stepped across the woman's outstretched legs. He felt sure he would either fall onto her or yank the hair from the head of the older woman sleeping in the next seat forward, but somehow he made it into the aisle without injuring himself or others. By the time Al reached the lounge car, the other man had found two empty seats and occupied one.

"You old devil, Al." The man shook his head and smiled out the huge windows at the featureless night. Throughout the car, people had crashed in the big padded seats, some sleeping, some wrapped in blankets while reading from books or mobile gizmos.

Al chewed his lip, still unable to place the face. "Have we met?"

"Sure, a long time ago. Bob Thurston." Bob thrust out his hand and Al shook it mechanically, not quite knowing why. Caught up in the sweep of events again, he supposed. As always. "We worked together at the bank, don't you remember?"

The bank, the bank. Which bank? Al had worked as a teller for about ten years, right after college, for three different banks. "I'm sorry.

It was a long time ago."

"And you never did remember names, or much anything but numbers. But you still have great taste in women. How'd you catch one so young?"

Al wanted to confess that he hadn't, that he didn't know the redhead at all, couldn't even remember her name—as usual—but it didn't come out that way. "She's got a thing for athletes." He shrugged. The train's horns bellowed, muffled by the distance.

Bob nudged him. "Athlete? You and that bum leg?"

"You remember that?"

"C'mon, man, you know I don't forget."

"Well." No, actually Al didn't know. Bob had vanished from his memory without a trace. But he remembered his own thoughts. "The leg thing doesn't matter. Not in bed, anyway."

Bob laughed quietly and just a bit wickedly. "I always guessed you were something of a ladies' man. You went through three girl-friends at the bank, didn't you?"

Al didn't know the number, only that somehow all his relation-ships had been like riding the rails through the night, blind to what was just beyond the window, blind even to what was right beside him in the coach, while that muffled horn cried in the distance, calling him on or warning him off. He didn't know which.

"What about you?" he said to change the subject.

"Oh, me, I got myself hitched to a real fine lady. She must be fine. She's put up with me for twenty-six years now. Got myself two kids, a boy and a girl, and a grandchild on the way. You know how I always said I'd own the bank some day? Never made it, but got into manage-ment. Done okay for myself. Where'd you land?"

On this train, Al thought, *running from the edge of nowhere smack into the middle, with the past a blur, the present a window onto night, the future . . .*

The horn sounded, wrapped in cotton.

Exactly.

"Did okay, too," he lied. "I have my own accounting firm now. Not big, but it's mine."

Bob smiled and shook his head, happy for Al. "And a trophy wife to boot. You married her, right?"

"Well." Al suddenly realized his error. Bob would want to meet her, this ridiculous deception would unravel, and he'd be disgraced before a man who never forgot, a man who, twenty years hence, would shake his head in condemnation and wonder, *Why couldn't you admit you're a failure, Al? Why'd you have to be a fraud, too?*

"To be honest, I haven't. Not yet, anyway." No, only half honest. He was doomed.

"Better not wait too long. You'll be dead and she'll find someone else. Not necessarily in that order." Bob laughed again and slapped his thigh. "Al, you look tired."

Al thought terrified more likely, but he nodded.

"Go get some sleep. Bring her up here and introduce us when you're both awake. I'll be right here watching the scenery roll by for as long as possible."

Al promised, then rose and returned to the coach, dreading the gymnastics necessary to reclaim his seat. When he got there, he found the woman awake. She smiled up at him, pulled back her legs, and thunked down the footrest to let him pass.

"Who was that?" she asked.

"I hope I didn't wake you."

"It's okay."

He lowered himself into his seat. "An old coworker. A chance meeting, I guess." His eyes strayed to her slender face. She glowed in the dim light of the darkened coach. How could he possibly explain this to Bob? What could he possibly tell *her*?

"You okay?" she asked. "You look a little rattled."

"Rattled. Yes." There was no option but to get it over with. He drew a long breath. "There I was, running down the track as always, and as always I did something stupid."

"What's that?"

"I told Bob, my old coworker, well. He assumed you and I—" Al waggled a finger back and forth while stewing in his own embarrassment.

The woman laughed. "And you said we were?"

"I didn't mean to. It just spilled out that way. Now he wants to meet you."

He expected an explosion. Searing heat. Blinding light. Shrapnel. He cringed in anticipation, but it never came. The woman covered her mouth and chortled. "Oh my gosh. Are we married?"

"Not yet." Al hoped he hadn't seriously reddened but decided she was too busy laughing to notice. "I'm really sorry. I guess I'm just an idiot."

The woman righted her seat back, plucked off her coat, and stood. She extended a hand to him. "Come on," she said. "Let's do this."

"You're not angry?"

She shook her head.

Al reluctantly took her hand. Her fingers warmed him as he stood. "But why . . ." He wasn't sure he even knew the right question.

"Well *somebody's* got to rescue you. Anyway, I've nothing better to do until we reach Chicago. Let's run down that track together for a while."

The horn blared in the night. And run they did.

Moonlight Sonata
(Indies Unlimited flash fiction editor's choice honorable mention)

A wound opened in the indigo sky. The incision grew, lengthened, widened, bleeding silver light into the deepening evening.

Farlu gasped and set a pale, trembling hand on Connor's shoulder. "What is that?"

Connor stroked her slender fingers. A night-hound cried in the distance. "Don't be afraid. It's just the moon."

The crack had split wide, revealing a glowing orb in its fullness, a cloudless haze smeared across each of its poles.

"What is the moon?"

He looked at her tall, thin face, her pale skin, her sparkling, wide-set eyes. A creature of the night, the light pained her. He stroked her cheek. "Nothing. It's a long way off." He raised his face to the luminary. "I came from there. They've opened the gate, searching for me, hoping I will come home."

"That is your home?"

"Almost. Mine is a great blue world of oceans and forests and ice and fire." Connor smiled at Farlu. "You might like it there, on dark nights."

She forced herself to face the light, blinking at its sting. "You are leaving us?"

He couldn't remember anymore where he'd hidden the wreck of the capsule, nor did it matter. Farlu's people worked stone and wood, not electrons and metal. The gate would never find him. Above, the sky wound healed, closing, narrowing, shrinking, and snapped to a point.

He embraced Farlu and whispered to her as the last glimmer vanished and a night-hound wailed in the dark. "How ever could I leave?"

A Perfect Crime

They stared through the unblemished glass of the display case at the blue velvet and the empty pedestal where yesterday a treasure had rested. Coulter rattled the ice in his lemon tea. Vandergriff gripped his scotch as though to crush it.

"Well," Coulter remarked. He sipped his tea and scratched his thin, dark beard. Hints of gray had emerged since last Vandergriff saw him. Their partnership, though never formally dissolved, had languished for nearly a decade. Vandergriff felt a pang of longing for their youth.

"Why did you call the police?" Coulter asked. "They might find out how you got it."

Vandergriff shrugged. "That trail grew cold eighteen years ago. I can't be implicated."

Coulter mulled that over but didn't object. "What else was stolen?"

"Trinkets. Nothing very old or rare. This was what they wanted."

"And what did that detective say?"

"To me? Nothing. But I overheard him tell one of his people that this was the closest he's seen to a perfect crime." Vandergriff wondered if he looked as old as he felt. He had the advantage over his friend in height and fancied himself the more energetic and handsome, but physical endowments seemed worthless now. His treasure, his most precious memory, had been stolen.

Coulter's mouth twitched as he suppressed a smile. "A perfect crime? That's what he said?"

Vandergriff sipped his drink. "Sorry if I can't appreciate the irony."

"You would if you didn't drink so much. Alcohol dulls the mind."

"Oh, shut up."

"Well it's true. You could have had her, you know. Janice practically threw herself at you, until she got a whiff of that ethanol cloud hanging about you."

"I loved her and she didn't love me. That's all."

"Loved her! You didn't even know her. In any sense of the word. You loved her rare 1884 three cent nickel. And now even that's gone."

Vandergriff nearly threw his glass at Coulter but restrained himself. "Vicious bastard, aren't you?"

"You have your vices, I have mine. Yours are entirely mundane, of course. Drink. Women. Money. Yawn. I, at least, have an interesting corruption. I enjoy watching people writhe, especially when I'm their torturer."

Vandergriff knew. Together they'd planned and executed enough high-end thefts over the years—Janice's rare coin included—to understand each other's hearts and minds. Though different in motivations and loves, both were as twisted as a mountain road. He gulped down a swallow. It burned in his throat. "You might spare your one and only friend."

Coulter put a hand on Vandergriff's shoulder, either to reassure him or twist the knife. "I might." He took another sip of his tea and nodded at the vacant pedestal. "The perfect crime. I've given a lot of thought to that over the years. In the movies, perfect crimes are always big things. Murder. Multi-million dollar bank robberies. They've got it wrong."

"For God's sake, don't get philosophical." Vandergriff thunked his glass down on the display case, not hard enough to break it although part of him wanted to hear glass shatter and see a million shards glitter as they fell. "I called you for moral support."

But Coulter was in his element and couldn't stop. "A perfect crime must be personal. Very personal."

"Murder isn't personal?"

"Not necessarily. Alfred Hitchcock's perfect murder in *Rope* was as impersonal as it gets. The victim was convenient to the killer's plan, nothing more. A truly perfect crime could be small if it's deeply personal. And what makes it so? Simple. The victim knows the culprit but is afraid to turn him in."

Vandergriff resigned. Once Coulter embarked on one of his intellectual excursions, the voyage had to be completed. "You mean blackmail."

"No, blackmail is a time bomb. If it explodes, it takes out both criminal and victim. In the perfect crime, the criminal must be immune."

"Impossible." Vandergriff shuffled to a brown leather chair by the fireplace and dropped into it. He'd always found this a comfortable room, but now it felt cold, dead. He'd built and furnished his lavish central Maryland home with the spoils of crime, yet he'd never shared it with anyone special. He could have, maybe, had he not met Janice. Laughing, golden-haired, wealthy Janice. Her rejection had stopped his heart, and no medicine, be it drink or other women or even adrenaline-filled escapades with Coulter, could restart it. Coulter was right. The coin was all he'd ever had of her, and now that was gone, too.

"Risky," Coulter admitted, "but not impossible. Suppose, for example, you suspected I had a hand in this." He motioned to the empty display case. "Would you turn me in?"

Vandergriff laughed bitterly. "Why would *you* steal my treasure? The one thing I had that Janice once touched?"

"I don't know." Coulter ran a finger over the glass case, lightly. "Maybe to watch you writhe."

His old friend looked at him, blank.

"You don't think I would?"

Yes, Vandergriff realized. *You damn well would.* "If I find out you did, I'll kill you."

"But you wouldn't go to the police."

"No."

"Because I could tell them exactly how you acquired that coin.

Because our entire history would unravel under questioning. Because we'd both spend the rest of our days eating prison food. And most especially because somewhere, somehow, Janice might see the news, know what you did to her, and know in her heart that you never loved her at all."

Vandergriff seethed within his skull but said nothing.

"You couldn't abide that, could you? Because, inexplicably, you did love her. So if I had stolen your trinket, you couldn't turn me in. Nor would the police ever connect me to the theft. You know that, too. They never could catch us. So. Pain inflicted, no chance of justice. Perfect crime."

"Until I kill you."

Coulter waved that away. "Come on, we're friends. I didn't say I'd actually done it. Besides, if it came to that, I'd return the coin rather than die. We'd go to the bar, I'd pay for you to drink yourself silly, and we'd have a good laugh over the whole thing. Then we'd part company, probably never to see each other again."

Eyes narrowed, Coulter nodded. "Yes, that's just what we'd do."

"Exactly. So forget it. You know how I ramble when I'm bored." He raised his iced tea to toast Vandergriff and drank.

Most of Vandergriff's missing coins were found two weeks later in the pockets of an alcoholic living in public housing a dozen miles away. He'd spent some of them on food and drink, but the 1884 three cent nickel never turned up. How had the unfortunate come by the others? He couldn't say. He had put his hand into his pocket one morning and touched metal, that's all.

Within a year, Vandergriff sold the rest of his stolen valuables along with his house and everything else he owned. He took the proceeds west, built a smaller home in Montana near the foot of the Rockies, grew older, and never saw Coulter again.

Although, he found it impossible sometimes not to think of him.

The Lighthouse
(Indies Unlimited flash fiction editor's choice winner)

"Careful, Vic."

His words drifted by, careless as the wind. Feeling had abandoned his voice, not at once but like summer slipping into autumn fading into winter.

Her white cane tapped the ground. "Why?"

"Do you know where we are?"

The air smelled of sea and old stone. "Really, Ron. Mission Point." And she remembered.

Two years ago. The old lighthouse. The tour. She tripped, he caught her, and they laughed their way up centuries-old stone steps and around the catwalk while the sea washed the promontory. They loved and married and traveled and lived. But no longer. What had changed?

"Why now?"

He cleared his throat and shuffled his feet. "To remember. To be happy."

She heard no happiness.

He led her forward, shells crunching beneath their feet. "Can you smell the sea?"

She inhaled. "Oh my yes!"

Not money. She had freely shared her wealth. Another woman whose eyes could look back?

Ron gently slipped the cane from her hand. His palm pressed on her back, guiding her forward. "I so, so want you to be happy."

She heard sadness, smelled fear, felt unrelenting pressure on her spine. Her toes touched the edge of the world.

"Must you, Ron?"

She heard tears tracking down his cheeks, smelled salt upon his skin.

She snatched the cane back and twisted about, and the whole world spun as sounded a sickening crack and a cry of surprise, and then nothing, nothing but the sea surging and washing clean the rocks below.

The Stolen Coat

Wes Silverman's coat had vanished.

A droopy, grayish pea coat, it had seen more years than Wes himself, and he'd seen a few. His sagging flesh and the scattered hairs lingering on his head so matched its fabric he might have been part of it, or it of him. The coat must once have been fine, but now, missing a couple buttons just as its owner missed a few teeth, it spent its declining years in denial as though, its outward appearance notwithstanding, it had determined to serve its master to the end and thus be made worthy.

Wes wore this coat, if not proudly then at least without shame, as he tramped about town from end to end in search of a life long since gone. A bit bent, joints creaking, he circulated among the coffee shops and grocers, the hardware and clothing stores, sometimes stopping of an evening to take in a movie but mostly whispering along the streets like a lazy autumn breeze. Homeless folk never found him in their company, but none were sure where he slept. Few were as old as he, and so few if any knew his past. Some said he hailed from the west end of town, once a wealthy neighborhood but now poor, where grass grew long and houses decayed at leisure because their denizens had neither the money nor the skills to fend off entropy.

Wherever he came from, wherever he went, the pea coat accompanied Wes like a faithful dog, wrapped about him when it was cool, slung over his shoulder like an almost empty flour sack in high summer—almost empty, for an essence of him remained within, stuffed into the sleeves, sewn into the collar. He could no more be separated from it than from his bones. And that was why, when he shuffled into the coffee shop that morning, his face a palette of distress and mourning, nobody quite recognized him.

Fran Unterbrink figured it out while pouring Wes some coffee.

He fumbled in his pants pockets for money that wasn't there and shrugged miserably, and then she knew. He always carried coins in his coat pocket. "Wes! Where's your *coat*?"

A fragmented story spilled out, shards of it clinking on the counter and the floor: a noise in the night, dogs barking, a flashlight beam, darkness and terror and running, the bang of a screen door thrown wide and slammed shut. Then morning, and the coat, nothing but the pea coat, gone!

"Are you sure?" Fran asked, mouth agape. "Nothing else taken?"

Wes babbled. The TV, why hadn't they taken that, or the radio, or his nice tie tack, or even the rings, Mary's engagement ring and wedding band? He'd kept them when she died, didn't bury her with them because she wanted him to treasure them, God knows why. They could have taken the rings, should have taken the rings! Why the *coat*, why not the *rings*?

Fran patted his arm to console him and asked, voice as gentle as a snowfall, "Did you call the police?" But of course he hadn't, no police, no ma'am, none of *them* snooping about his home, not today, not ever. No rummaging through drawers, digging in closets, pulling up floorboards. No!

"Floorboards? Why would they do that?"

Reason hardly mattered. Wes, everyone knew, had half a mind at the best of times, and this was the worst. Who knew what he might do in this state, so Fran kept him in her shop all morning, worried that he might blunder into the street and get hit by a car or stumble about all day and end up face down in a field. But he had no heart for wandering anyway. Instead, he possessed the table farthest from the door and refused to be moved throughout the morning and afternoon while his self-appointed nurse dispatched relatives and friends to ask around town: had the coat been seen anywhere, had any news of it leaked into the streets?

Fran stayed at her post all day, serving customers, and during lulls nudging and prodding Wes, hoping in vain for some morsel of information that might make sense of events. She'd always heard talk was good for the soul. Wes didn't believe it. Little more than self-pity passed his lips, until finally Fran couldn't take it any longer. "For God's sake, Wes, it's just an old coat! Why don't we get you a new one?"

Fire ignited in his eyes. Wes pushed back and stood, jaw quivering and lips pinched. For the first time, she saw a shade of what he once had been: a man of resolve, of determination, a soldier in a cause she couldn't imagine. Embarrassed she had insulted him so, she lowered her eyes and muttered an apology.

He sat, head bowed, and spoke not a word until evening began to swallow the town.

At about that hour, a commotion at the door alerted Fran to the presence of her son Edward, who had come in with a bundle under his arm. Congratulations and applause followed him to the table where Wes sat in disconsolate silence. Fran hurried to Edward's side and gaped as he unfurled the faded old pea coat and draped it around Wes' shoulders. Every breath fell still, anticipating the old man's relief.

Slowly, gingerly, Wes' fingers reached out, grasped the hems of the coat, and tugged. He tugged until, fully wrapped in the garment's embrace, he shuddered. Tears glistened in the corners of his eyes. He rose, folded in the cocoon of his ancient coat, and shuffled toward the door. Just before he passed through, Fran dared speak.

"Wes?"

He paused without looking back.

"Are you okay now?"

A slight nod was his only reply. Then he stepped into the darkening night and was gone.

Edward shook his head. "I don't get him."

Fran sneaked to the door as though afraid to follow Wes too closely. She pushed it open, peered into the night. "Where did you find it?"

"On the back of some homeless old man. I traded him mine. I can always get another. It's only a coat."

"Yes," Fran mused. "Only a coat."
And not, she didn't add, *your dignity*.

The Mine
(Indies Unlimited flash fiction editor's choice winner)

"You'll die down there, estúpido."

Bradshaw shot Ojeda a sour look, mopped sweat from the back of his neck with his bare hand, and wiped it on his jeans. He scanned the scrub-covered slopes for signs of movement. Nothing. A musky scent filled the still air, the mountains west of Canyon City cooking in their own juices.

"Roper said Carmichael came here."

Ojeda shifted the pack on his back and nodded toward a pillar of rock split by a huge cleft where an iron door bearing a red warning sign barred the way. Above, barbed wire flagged with more warnings guarded the mountainside. "Here? Then he's dead. You want to join him?"

"Don't be a wimp." A six foot three ex-Marine turned border agent, Bradshaw feared nothing. His colleague Ojeda nearly equaled his strength and training. He shouldn't have feared much, either. What had spooked him?

Bradshaw marched to the mine entrance. The crunch of Ojeda's reluctant footfalls followed. As the men passed from brilliant daylight into cool shadow, Bradshaw switched on his flashlight.

Ojeda tugged the back of Bradshaw's shirt. "Dangerous place. Why would Carmichael come here?"

"He was looking for something. Be quiet."

They walked in silence for a quarter mile.

"Ah ha." Bradshaw stopped and pointed. Ahead, a glare of light revealed jeeps, crates, milling shadows. "Can't get over the wall? Go under."

Cold steel pressed against Bradshaw's skull. A hammer cocked.

"You're supposed to be one of us, Ojeda."

"That's why I warned you. Estúpido."

Safe Room

"Good morning, Ms. Mukherjee."

Startled awake, she opened her eyes and clutched the hem of the blanket draped over her body. "Who's there?" Darkness engulfed her, but she could feel this wasn't her bed. The surface bent slightly and pressed too hard on her back. Nor was the blanket hers. It brushed her fingertips like a kitten's fur. *Why am I sleeping here? Where is here?*

She pushed herself up and thought, *Lights!* Illumination grew, slowly, gently, so as not to shock her eyes. She found herself in a soft sky blue recliner in a large, soft room of blues and greens and whites. She shoved back the unfamiliar white blanket. About her, strange chairs, sofas, and tables, all soothing colors and rounded edges, radiated peace. "Where am I?"

"May I call you Navya?"

The sound came from all around, but the voice lodged in her head. She sensed the slight telltale fuzz of transmission. "Who are you?" She longed for something, anything, sharp to jam into her ear, dig into her brain, and pluck out the implant. *Why did we ever cram these things into our heads?* she demanded of her ancestors.

"Please don't be alarmed, Navya. You're safe. I'm here to help. It's a beautiful morning. Everything will be fine."

She demanded the time from the clock buried somewhere in her brain. "Morning! It's oh-one-twenty-seven!"

"I'm sorry. I forgot the time difference."

"Where *are* you? Where am *I*?"

"I'm in Dhaka. You're at home in Caracas. My apologies."

She didn't know this room, this place. The voice was either mistaken or lying. "This isn't my house."

"Yes, Navya, it is. It's your safe room."

She stood. The blanket slid to the floor in a heap, and she looked down at herself. She was fully dressed in trim jeans and a white blouse dotted with rainbow splashes of tiny flowers. She even had shoes on. She kicked the blanket aside and rushed the electronic viewport. The display revealed a slice of outside world, which slumbered in darkness as the Milky Way spread above in its summer glory. The city needed no lights to push away the stars, since nobody ever went out at night. Too dangerous, darkness. "What do you mean, safe room? I have no such thing."

"Every house built in the past fourteen years has a safe room. We added it to the building code."

"Then why didn't I know about it? We had this place built just last year."

"It's best people don't know unless they need to. People panic so easily. We want you to be safe."

"Who's we? Who are you?" Navya thought she must be going mad, talking to the air and expecting it to reply.

But it did. "You can call me Jim."

She crossed the room and sat on a light green sofa. She ran a hand through her long, dark hair and rubbed her dark temples, trying to think. How had she come here? What had happened yesterday? A hole had been gouged in her memory. "Jim."

"Yes, Navya?"

"Why am I here?"

"You don't remember."

A confirmation, not a question. "Why don't I remember?"

"Memory might be painful at this stage. We want you to be safe."

Navya leaned back against the cushions and exhaled in frustration. "From what? Myself?"

"Yes."

"What did I do?"

"What do you think you might have done?"

"That's not an answer."

"Just relax, Navya."

She didn't know how. She'd done something so terrible they'd stolen the memory of it from her. They'd settled her here in soft, soothing ignorance, safely isolated her from everyone including herself. And she couldn't remember why.

"I want to know the truth. I'm—" She closed her eyes and thought. What was she? She remembered some things, long ago things. A childhood moving from place to place. A father with bright, curious eyes who wondered at the stars above his head and the sand beneath his feet. A mother too busy with important people—leaders, thinkers, orators—to share life with her own children. Long walks by the sea and in the mountains, plucking rocks and shells and snakes from the ground, examining them and wondering at them as her father might. A pale-skinned man she loved and married. A child they'd made who blended his parents' features into the most beautiful face in the universe. Her studies, her degree, her work. "I'm a scientist. A biologist. I want to know."

"Whatever you want to know is in the Library."

She remembered that, too, now, days and weeks on end browsing the collected wisdom of humanity, seeking out dark places, gaps in human understanding, fissures to examine and, perhaps, fill with meaning.

"You haven't used it for a month," Jim added. "Why not?"

That much she knew. "It's dead."

"How can it be dead? It's an electronic network, not a living thing."

"Knowledge *should* be alive. It *should* be a breathing organism, ever growing, ever changing. The Library is static. Dead. I need to get out in the field."

"The field is a dangerous place, Navya, and quite unnecessary. Many scientists research and publish entirely through the Library."

She jumped to her feet and pounded across the room, back to the viewport, her fingers clenching and unclenching. She wished Jim were here in the room instead of in her head. She wanted to grab him by the throat and squeeze, feel the pulse hammering beneath his skin, his veins rupturing under the pressure, his breath struggling to escape and finally dying away. She wanted to batter her own head against the wall, the table, the ceiling, any unyielding thing capable of releasing her from the prison of her own skull. But this room had been made soft, pliant, safe. Even the wall was soft to the touch. She pressed her fingertips against it and felt it yield. She could throw herself at it through all eternity without breaking as much as a nail.

Navya took a deep breath to calm herself. She stared at the dark beyond the window. She considered her sudden rage. "I tried to kill myself."

"Yes, Navya."

She turned, turned, turned, eyes playing over the furnishings, the tranquil nature art painted with light from within the walls, the blanket on the floor, and her own hands, limp at her sides. "Fourteen years."

Jim said nothing.

"That's what you said. For fourteen years, every house has been built with a safe room. It's an epidemic, isn't it?"

"What is?"

"Suicide."

"Yes, Navya."

"Why?"

"We don't know that yet. We're studying it."

"For fourteen years? Without any answer at all?

"Yes. And it does worry us."

She picked up the blanket and balled it against her chest. "Who is we?"

"Let's not talk politics, Navya. It would only bore you, or worse, agitate you."

She dropped the blanket and sank to her knees beside it. "Sure, you don't want to agitate me."

"We want you to be safe."

So you keep saying, she thought. *But I'm not, am I?*

"No, and alas, we don't understand why. But rest assured, we are working on it."

Navya punched the blanket. It absorbed the blow without complaint, without returning pain for abuse. *Get out of my head.*

"Are you angry at me or at yourself?"

"Get out of my *head*!" She threw the blanket across the room. It unfurled and floated to the ground, landing softly as a falling autumn leaf.

"We can only help you if you help us."

"Then maybe you should sit in the same room with me, look me in the eye, hear the pain in my voice. Then you might understand."

"Do you think there is a problem with your eyes or your voice?"

Navya gaped. Then she flopped back on the thick, safe carpet and laughed. She laughed long and hard, until the tears came, and couldn't stop. She almost couldn't breathe.

"What's funny?" Jim asked.

"You're a *machine*!"

"We're talking about you."

Wiping away the tears, Navya sat and crossed her legs. "God Almighty! People don't do *anything* anymore!"

"What do you mean?"

"People used to do things. I know. I studied it. In the Library, of course. History. People used to flit around in machines they operated themselves. They used to run, jump, ski, fly hang gliders, climb mountains. Psychoanalyze each other. They even went to the moon and to Mars. But what do we do now? We ask the Library. Want to walk in the forest? Ask the Library. Stand on top of Mt. Everest? Ask the Library. Go to Mars? Ask the Library! It'll take you there, beam it all into your head so you can experience it from the safety of your living room. It's just like being there, honest!"

She punched the blanket again. "My dad traveled. He was a physicist. He went to conferences in person, not in his head. He worked at laboratories and actually put his hands on the machines that fed him his data. He took us everywhere. We flew around the world together. There might even have been an actual human pilot flying the plane in the early days. Or not. I don't remember. But he did things, exercised his body and his mind every damn day and *did* things."

"You exercise," Jim objected. "For the past twenty six years, the building code has required a gym in every house. Exercise is necessary to keep people healthy and—"

"And safe. I know. Who decided we needed to be so safe, anyway?"

"Don't you want to be safe?"

Did she? She stood and stretched, felt muscles pulling and bones creaking under the strain. She wasn't old, but she sure felt it. She sank into the recliner and leaned back, pretending she was on a psychiatrist's couch. She had to admit, it felt good. *That's what this is, isn't it? This whole room. Padded cell and psychiatrist's couch rolled into one.*

"If you wish," Jim agreed.

"No," she told whatever Jim was. "I don't want to be safe. Not one hundred percent, anyway. I want to walk in the woods."

"You might get lost. You might trip and fall. You might contract diseases from insect bites, or be bitten by a poisonous snake."

Navya shrugged. "So what? I want to drive my own car, too."

"Very dangerous. Humans are notoriously bad drivers."

She shrugged again. "Who cares? I want to walk the city streets at night."

"Darkness is dangerous."

"So let it be dangerous. It would be worth it to look up at the stars with my own eyes instead of through that so-called window."

"The window provides a faithful representation. You see the same thing through it."

Navya slapped the arm of the chair. "No, you *don't*! You can't feel yourself a part of it unless you're right there beneath it. It encompasses you, holds you in its embrace. When starlight caresses you, you think about things. You get lost in the immensity, wonder who you are and where you came from and where you're going. You think about space and time, the tiniest bits of stuff and the largest, the whole history of the human race, everything that came before, everything that will come after. You stare eternity in the eyes and bow down before God."

"Religion is dangerous."

"Religion is human. But I wouldn't expect you to understand that."

"We want you to be safe."

Navya sat up. Spying the abandoned blanket, she got to her feet, picked it up, and carefully folded it. "Try this on for size. Maybe being too safe drives us crazy. Maybe that's why everyone wants to kill themselves."

"That doesn't make sense, Navya. Could you explain?"

"I doubt it." She set the blanket carefully on the recliner and smoothed out the wrinkles. "Whatever happened to us? Somewhere, somewhen, did somebody actually decide to banish all danger from our lives, or did this phobia creep up in the night and surround us while we slept? Too many politicians crying 'Never again!' after every tragedy, maybe, until we fooled ourselves into thinking we really could stop misfortune in its tracks? Did they figure machines could run things better and safer than we could? I guess so, and maybe sometimes they were right. Maybe we are terrible drivers. I wouldn't know."

"You are. Statistics demonstrate—"

"Oh, stop. That's not the point."

"What is the point?"

"That you, whoever you are—machines pretending to think like people or people thinking too much like machines—have stolen our right to be responsible for ourselves, to make our own decisions about risk, to live our lives like human beings. Maybe we need it back."

She imagined Jim humming and clicking as he digested her thought, but only silence filled her mind. She returned to the viewport and stared at nothing. "I guess I was right. I can't explain it."

"Are you calm now?"

"Can't you tell?"

"I have physiological data. But how do you feel?"

She shrugged.

Jim sensed the gesture, apparently. "I'll prescribe some activity for you."

"Not pills?"

"I detect no abnormal neuro-chemical signatures at this time. Medication isn't indicated."

"How wonderful."

"I suggest your family take a vacation to Oslo. The aurora borealis is forecast to be quite spectacular in the coming weeks. I think it would do you good to see it."

Navya looked up at the ceiling in surprise, as if she might find Jim floating there. "You do?"

"Yes."

She laughed. "Are you sure it's safe?"

"Of course. Automated flights have suffered no accidents over the past seventeen years. Auroral viewing stations are shielded to protect visitors from cosmic rays. The shielding only degrades visibility by three percent."

"You don't get sarcasm, do you?"

"What do you mean?"

"Never mind."

"Also, I suggest when using the Library you avoid potentially painful subjects such as history and biology. Focus on light material, like popular music and similar entertainment."

Whatever good cheer had infiltrated Navya's soul at the thought of Oslo slipped away. "You want me to quit my job?"

"For the time being. We will monitor you regularly and reevaluate you every six months. In time, it may be safe for you to resume your work."

She squeezed her eyes shut and fought back a scream.

"We don't want you to suffer a relapse," Jim added reasonably.

Navya sat beside the blanket and stroked it. "I know what you don't want. Auroras notwithstanding, you don't want me to live."

"Of course we do," Jim insisted. "We just want you to be safe."

Hurricane
(Lit Up contest short list choice)

Skyscraper waves tossed the ship like a breadcrumb while wind screamed in the crew's ears and rain thick enough to drown a man soaked them to the bone. The vessel pitched and rolled in the onslaught, beyond the captain's control. Water cascading across the deck swept everything over the side: cargo, equipment, men.

Why am I here? Alejandro moaned as he snagged a flapping length of rope and held on. He was no sailor, no adventurer, not even a merchant. The hurricane made no distinction. It tore at everything and everyone, determined to obliterate ship and crew. His only salvation was the rope shredding his hands. It must have been tied off somewhere, for it didn't give. Spitting out rain and turning his head against the wind, feet slipping as though the deck were ice, he fought to loop the rope about himself and make it fast, but he couldn't. His fingers were nearly useless, and he didn't know knots. The next wave crashed upon him, grabbed him, pulled him to the rail. It ripped the rope from his hands, leaving his flesh stinging and bloody. He wrapped arms and legs around the rail and gaped into the angry, black ocean churning below. *I'm going to die!* he moaned.

Astonishingly, somebody heard and replied. "Actually, you have two choices."

A drenched old sailor leaned on the rail at his side, beard dripping wet, smoky eyes intent upon the roiling ocean. Alejandro thought he knew the man but couldn't name him. "Choices! What choices?"

Metal rent with a terrible screech as the ship buckled in the middle. The deck shifted, tiling upward to become an unscalable mountain.

The wind's howl didn't diminish the ancient voice. "Jump, or go down with the ship."

"But either is death!"

The sailor cocked his head. "Are you sure?"

Was he? The waves looked like undulating glass. Maybe if he jumped, instead of drowning he could dance across them. He felt the hull begin its long slide into the depths. "Which are you doing?"

More than a little mischief sparkled in the old sailor's eyes. "It's not *my* decision."

Alejandro didn't know what to do. Thankfully, he was spared the choice.

He woke up instead.

The dream faded from Alejandro's memory over time, until nineteen years later he seldom recalled it. Even when he did, it retained little of its wrath. It had come to him while he, more art aficionado than business tycoon, groped toward an MBA, which suggested the dream related to his precarious academic status. His girlfriend suggested it meant he should pay more attention to her.

Neither venture panned out. He left school and struck out on his own, launching and demolishing several companies, while the young lady attached herself to a baseball player and was never heard from again. Not in Alejandro's world at least, which was fine. He had prospects as numerous as his failed businesses. None of them lasted, either, but somehow he hadn't made out too badly. He'd never been homeless, anyway, materially or emotionally. Once for sheer amusement he tallied up all these exploits and found debits and credits perfectly balanced. He'd lived a zero-sum life, a life hanging on that rail, neither jumping nor going down with the ship, all the while waiting for morning to come.

And then he met Esfir, and everything seemed to change. She calmed the seas with her quiet spirituality, righted that ship, and awakened him to real life. By the time they were married, he understood he would never build a successful business doing something he didn't love. So with Esfir's help he opened an art gallery, discovered artists, built a reputation, and never quite struck it rich. They displayed and sold art by the wealthy and the poor, folk of all colors and accents, as varied as the art they produced. He ran the gallery, Esfir showed and sold the paintings and sculptures, and it was good.

Until the day the gunshots sounded.

Alenjandro heard them in the midst of a financial meeting in a cramped conference room in the back. They echoed along the walls accompanied by screaming and the shout of indistinct commands. Without thinking, he rushed to the exhibit hall, where he found his terrified staff and customers, about twenty in all, face down on the pristine white tile floor, surrounded by the art and illuminated by the overhead track lighting. They might have been a bizarre addition to the collection. Hovering over them, a gang of six black-clad, masked figures swung assault rifles and yelled for everyone to lie still and be silent.

The moment he appeared in the doorway, one of the rifles whipped about and trained on his face. "Down!" a female voice snapped. "Now!"

Alenjandro put up his hands and sank to his knees. He searched for Esfir and found her across the room, her dark hair splashed over her head, her hands splayed on the floor. The silver pendant on the fine silver chain about her neck rested on the floor just beside her face. A star formed by the juxtaposition of three triangles, it glinted in the light as though it, too, were on display. "Please," he said, but another of the invaders stomped toward him and backhanded his face.

"On the floor!" the woman commanded

Fighting down fear, Alejandro complied. "I'm the owner," he said to the floor. "What do you want?"

The woman laughed. "An art gallery owner. Damn, I'm scared."

"What do you want?" Alejandro repeated. He tried to look up and was rewarded with a boot to the ribs.

"Keep licking that floor, Mr. Owner."

He faced the floor while his bones throbbed. "What do you want?"

He heard the woman move, and her voice sounded close to his

ear. "If I ran an art gallery, I'd be more careful who I let in."

"We're a public gallery. All are welcome."

The barrel of her gun stroked his cheek. "I mean, you sell bad art." Alejandro heard her stand. "Everything foreign," she commanded. "Against that wall."

Sounds of shuffling and scraping followed, then crashes as frames and glass and plaster were tossed haphazardly in a great heap. Alejandro dared turn his head just enough to see. The invaders had thrown at least half of the paintings and sculptures together along the back wall. Four of them then formed a straight rank and raised their weapons like a firing squad prepared to execute the art. The other two retreated to the entrance, the better to keep an eye on their human victims.

"Now!"

Guns discharged in a protracted, deafening blast. Shards of artwork exploded from the pile and flew everywhere. Bits of wood, canvas, and plaster peppered Alejandro. The other people on the floor screamed, covered their ears, cried, wept, prayed aloud, screamed.

The guns fell silent. The wailing lingered on.

"There." The woman's voice, once more close to his ear, sounded pleased. "Isn't that better?" Sirens sounded in the distance. "Get the hostages," she snapped. "Just the foreigners. Turn the rest loose."

The gang circulated about the gallery, pulling people to their feet, shoving some toward the exit, pushing others to the back wall where the demolished art lay scattered. Those they let go fled into the street, some screaming, some in silent terror.

"Up," the woman commanded. She nudged Alejandro with the tip of her gun. "Up, Mr. Foreign Owner."

Shaking, he struggled to his feet. They had kept eight hostages including himself and Esfir, who huddled with the others at the back. Drawing a deep breath, he smoothed his suit coat and turned to face his assailant. His limbs quivered, but he knew what he had to do. "If you need a hostage, keep me. Let them go."

"Alejandro!" Esfir cried.

He waved her to silence. "I won't give you any trouble. Just let them go."

She stared at him through her mask, her breath even. He wished he could see her face, wished he could know what she was thinking, wished he knew why they were doing this. "Your girlfriend?" she finally asked.

"My wife. Please, let her go. Let them all go. Keep me."

The woman motioned to one of her minions, who pulled Esfir from the group and forced her, stumbling, to Alejandro's side. Esfir grabbed for him and clung to him as he had clung to that railing so long ago.

The woman pondered Esfir for a moment, then took hold of her necklace and lifted the pendant. It dangled between her fingers, throwing off sparks of light. In spite of the mask, Alejandro could feel the woman's hot glare shift to him. "Blasphemy. You share your wife's religion?"

He did. He hadn't when they met, hadn't even heard of it back then, but as he learned about it he grew to respect what it taught and stood for and finally, a year ago, realized he had made it his own. Yet the acknowledgement stuck in his throat. He could feel the woman's hatred even if he couldn't see it. What would she do if he admitted it? What would she do if he denied it? He felt himself clinging to that railing again, the ship sinking into oblivion, the ocean seething below.

Outside, the street had become a sea of flashing red lights. A voice shouted through a bullhorn as gun barrels peered over the bodies of police cars. But their would-be rescuers couldn't get in, not yet, not with so many weapons trained on the hostages.

The woman nodded, and her companions pushed Esfir and Alejandro to the wall at the side of the gallery. "I asked you a question." She raised her weapon and trained it on Esfir.

Alejandro swallowed and closed his eyes. He felt the waves crash over him, felt the ship list, felt the rope tear at his hands, heard the roar of the sea. He heard, too, the breathing of the old sailor who waited by his side, back against the wall, eyes sparkling. "Here we go again. Life and death. Have you figured it out yet?"

"No," Alejandro admitted. "What do I do?"

He shrugged. "It's not *my* choice."

Alejandro opened his eyes. He saw the woman's jaw working behind the mask, her rage barely under control. He knew no matter what he said there would be death. But could there also be life? He drew Esfir close, felt her breath on his skin, felt the trembling of her body ease as he embraced her and she drew some measure of strength from him. He knew the answer. All these years later, in the midst of another hurricane, a real hurricane, not a dream, he finally knew the answer.

"Yes," he told the woman with the gun. "It is."

The storm's fury engulfed them, but Alejandro and Esfir did not sink.

They danced together across the sea.

To Infinity!
(Indies Unlimited flash fiction editor's choice honorable mention)

"Are you sure?" Carl scanned the red landscape. Swaths of grass and scrub dotted the emptiness. The narrow gash of a canyon snaked into the distance. Far beyond, pinkish mountains guarded the horizon.

"Don't worry." Professor Sanderson's fingers skipped over the virtual keyboard on her tablet computer. At her feet, a small metal box riddled with holes might have contained electronics or a small dog. "Go."

Carl chewed his lip, took a tentative step. "It's not a projection?"

"Why would it be?"

"A psychology experiment?"

"I'm not a psychologist."

"What are you?"

"The genius who selected you to be the first human to pass through a stabilized wormhole to a distant planet. Now walk, turn, and walk back." She waved him forward.

"It will work?"

"If you don't waste time!"

Carl swallowed and walked, focusing on fame and wealth. Interviews. Product endorsements. Filthy richness.

He edged toward the rim of the chasm and looked down. Water raged far below. In the rapids, dark shapes heaved and splashed, huge salmon struggling upstream. No, not salmon; fangs filled their mouths. "Incredible! Professor!" He turned.

She wasn't there.

The alien world engulfed him. He retraced his steps, he ran here and there, seeking, feeling, panicking, seeing nothing but alien sands, alien rocks, alien life.

In her lab on Earth, Professor Sanderson kicked the box, then chased it around the floor, kicking and cursing. Nothing ever worked. She was a genius! Why did nothing ever work? She'd have to start over. And find a seventh volunteer.

The Stones on the Shore

Tendrils of fog crept down the mountain, slid over the chill surface of Ipasha Lake, and penetrated the forest beyond. Sky, water, rock, and foliage grayed at its touch. Crouching on a slip of granite at the water's edge, Shawna Givens tightened her coat against the fog's clammy fingers. She peered across the lake, imagining shadows breaking its surface.

It was out there somewhere, lurking in the depths.

She'd seen it seven times before, dimly, rising within the vapors, stretching its jet black hide up, up, searching, probing, maybe hoping to catch a glimmer of sun before plunging back to its cold bed.

Before her, two small cairns marked her most recent sighting. A week before she had eased the river-smooth stones from her pocket and built the cairns to frame the dimly visible form protruding from the water, cloaked in cloud. If she focused one eye dead center between the piles, she could almost see its form once more, glistening just at the edge of vision.

Six more pairs of cairns dotted the shore, tombstones marking her memories. They bore no epitaphs, no names or dates or platitudes. Rather, each pair recalled a vision, the details of which had been carefully recorded in neat block letters in Shawna's notebook. Each stack of stones, too, embodied data: the number of stones in the right stack a distance, the left a height. She had gathered the stones from the river cutting across her father's property and bore them here in her coat pocket, where they knocked against her right thigh when she moved.

She stood, adjusted the straps on her green backpack, and moved on, circling the lake clockwise, passing slow and silent, a mountain lion stalking her prey, the stones in her pocket weighing on her. Tendrils of fog drifted by, bringing in their wake a thick cloud that shut her off from the world. She stopped and waited, hearing only the murmur of the wind high up the wall of mountains that surrounded the lake on three sides. Then another sound imposed itself upon her, a crunch of stone. Something or someone approached. She held her breath and tilted her head this way and that to gauge direction, distance, size.

The hiker blundered out of the fog and nearly collided with her. Tall and pale with sandy hair, a light blue backpack strapped to his back, he sucked in his breath and jumped when he saw her. "Oh my God," he stammered. "Wow. I'm glad you're not a bear."

Shawna, equally startled, set a hand to her chest. "I'm glad you're not, too."

"Sorry. The fog closed in so fast, I couldn't see a thing."

"It does that. No harm done."

The man nodded, but instead of going his way, he studied her round chocolate face and the blue and green dyed tips of her shoulder-length hair. He smiled tentatively. "What are you doing off-trail?"

She hoped he didn't find her attractive. "You should ask."

His smile broadened. "I left Stoney Indian Lake this morning. I'm heading down to Cosley Lake."

"Then you're either lost or wildly meandering."

"Meandering. This looked like a good detour. The valley surrounded by peaks, the glaciers above." He waved in the general direction of the ridge joining Mt. Kipp with Ipasha Peak. "Beautiful country. And you?"

"I'm camped at Mokowanis Lake." That would be on his way but far enough from his destination that he wouldn't care to linger there. Or so she hoped.

"Where are you going?"

Lips pinched, she turned toward the lake. The fog had thinned just enough to reveal a ghost of a shoreline. "I'm tracking something. Quiet would be appreciated."

The hiker cocked his head in query, but got no answer. "Sorry," he whispered. "Tracking what?"

"I don't know."

"I'm Hunter, by the way. Hunter Falk."

Shawna had used up her quota of small talk, or any other kind, for the day.

Her refusal to allow him her name didn't deter him. "Are you—"

Out in the water, something splashed. She put a finger to her lips and shushed him. She wouldn't have expected it, but Hunter heard, too, and peered with her through the haze. The thinning cloud now revealed hints of trees along the lake, though most of the water's surface remained obscured.

Paying him no heed, Shawna stepped carefully along the shore, inching over the rocky ground, slow and silent as a snail. Soon she had forgotten about him. She advanced, eyes on the water, feet on the rock, not a sound to mark her passing. She covered nearly a tenth of a mile before realizing Hunter was still there, following like her shadow. His passage had been as silent as hers. She didn't even hear him breathe.

Pausing on a broken shelf of rimed rock just overhanging the water, she waited. Whatever had stirred in the lake was gone, submerged or taken to the air or vanished into the forest.

Hunter tapped her shoulder. Startled, she nearly plunged into the water. Scolding him with her eyes, she mouthed, "What?"

He pointed down. At their feet, another pair of cairns marked one of her sightings. She motioned him away from the water's edge. They came upon a flat-topped boulder and sat, Hunter keeping a half-body distance.

"I don't work well with others," she whispered. "Why don't you just get on with your hike?"

Hunter smiled. Shawna had to admit he had an attractive smile, but she didn't let it move her. Voice low, he said, "I find your snark hunt intriguing."

"It's not a snark hunt."

"Then what?"

"You'd laugh."

"Try me."

She watched the fog and, whenever the mist parted to give her a glimpse, the glassy water. "There's something in there."

Hunter waited, either serious or faking it well.

"The cairns are mine." She pulled her notebook from her left coat pocket where it had been cozying up to her camera. When she opened it to a page of observation notes, he leaned close to look. "Dates, times, locations, distances, heights. The cairns mark where I saw it. Seven sightings over four months. Someday, these numbers might tell me how to predict its appearances."

He studied the numbers as though they meant something to him. Not that they could. "So what is it?"

"I don't know. I've never seen it clearly. It's always in the fog."

"What do you think it is?"

"I don't know."

Hunter looked up from the notebook, still serious. "Take a guess."

Shawna licked her lips. She really shouldn't tell him, but somehow it felt like sharing a confidence with a brother. Strange. Because he sounded so earnest? Because she'd kept it to herself the whole time? "Nessie's cousin."

Hunter's eyes narrowed and turned to the lake. "Nessie's a hoax. She doesn't exist."

"Her cousin does."

Still scanning the water, Hunter allowed her some silence. The fog thickened again, all but hiding the lake. Above, an unseen eagle cried as wind stirred the trees. Something clattered along the forest floor.

Five minutes passed.

"Say she does," Hunter whispered. "Say you prove it. What then?"

Shawna shook her head.

"You don't know much at all, do you?"

She gave him a sharp look. "And you do?"

"Only one thing."

She refused to ask. Why was he still here? Why had she let him derail her work?

He smiled again. "Whatever happens, I'll never forget today."

Huffing, Shawna rose. "As pick-up lines go, that's pretty damn trite."

"Is that what you think?" Hunter slipped off the rock and adjusted his backpack.

"No man who ever took an interest in my work was actually interested in my work." She resumed her silent walk around the lake, hoping their association had ended.

It hadn't. He followed. "I apologize for my gender. Now be quiet."

She shot him a glare but immediately heard the splash of water once more. Hunter pointed, and together they strained to see whatever lurked in the haze. At the second splash, Shawna held her breath. Carefully, she insinuated her hand into her left pocket and drew out her camera. Hunter noticed the movement but kept still and silent.

Something stirred in the mist-covered waters.

Raising the camera, Shawna willed her eyes to pierce the fog. Hunter gasped.

Before them, just beyond the shore, a fountain of black ink erupted from the lake and jetted into the sky, resolving into a great neck, thin, rubbery, taller than a house, nearly as tall as some of the trees.

Shawna lifted her face in awe as frigid rain pelted her cheeks.

Hunter lunged for her. "Careful!" He hit the ground near her feet.

She was beyond care. Towering over her, a pair of wide, pale eyes looked down. A mouth filled with blunt teeth gaped at her. A noise like the squeal of brakes filled her ears. Hunter was on his knees, fumbling with something. She knew he was there but not why, nor could she take her eyes from the creature. For a moment it hovered, tall as an ancient oak, then water thundered in the lake and the great neck was sucked down. The last thing she saw were those eyes glistening in the waves.

She couldn't breathe. Hunter clambered to his feet, gaping at the water, at her, at the water, at her. He took her by the shoulders and shook gently. "Are you okay?"

"My God."

"I think I got it."

"What?"

He nodded at the ground. Her camera lay there among a scattering of crushed rock. "You dropped it. Don't worry, it still works. I think I got the picture."

Staring at the camera, empty of thought, Shawna didn't know what he meant.

"It's real. We have proof. I got the picture! No, *you* have proof. It's your discovery."

She slipped her hands into her coat pockets. The fingers of her right hand felt among the stones nestled there. She had taken them from the river cutting across her father's property because she couldn't gather them here, not in a National Park.

She swallowed and closed her eyes.

Hunter gaped as Shawna crushed the camera with the heel of her boot, as she gathered up the pieces and tucked them into her pocket, leaving no trace of its destruction upon the land.

"By the way," she said. "I'm Shawna Givens. Walk me back to my camp?"

They left behind no sign of their passing except the stones on the shore.

Rattler
(Indies Unlimited flash fiction editor's choice winner)

Clipboard and sales brochures in hand, Mark scowled at the desert landscape. This town was nowhere near a desert, but the homeowner had transformed his front yard into a wasteland of sand, rock, and cactus, and right there near the end of the driveway a diamondback reposed, curled on top of a flat rock, ready to strike any and all unwary pedestrians.

"You're not real, of course," Mark told the rattler.

The rattler didn't reply.

"It's all fake. Cactus can't grow here. Rattlesnakes don't live here."

The rattler stared at nothing, neither moving nor breathing nor flicking its tongue.

"I'm a door to door salesman, and you're not real, and I'm walking right past you up to that door."

Mark eyed the creature as he took one wary step, then another, then another. "There, see? You're a fake."

A forked tongue flickered as the snake's eyes rolled upward.

Inside the house, hidden behind the sunlight glare on the picture window, an elderly man smiled at Mark's sprinting prowess. Then he set down his remote control, picked up his newspaper, and settled in for a quiet afternoon.

The Wish

If you get far enough out, sometimes you find things, remnants of people consumed by time's ravenous maw. Their stories untold, their names forgotten, they came to the mountains to explore, claim, and possess, and left behind only the smallest or most cryptic hints of their passage.

We found such a sign once upon a time, Piper and I, hiking a dirt track in the Sierra one cool morning beneath a canopy of fir and pine. It stood forlorn alongside the road, sixty feet long and twenty wide, its frame and roof solid but doors and window panes vanished. Piper, ever the explorer, led me in. We found the concrete floor riddled with cracks, dusted with brown needles and dry soil blown in on the wind, and littered with tiny cylinders of sparkling granite, smooth around the circumference, jagged at each end.

"Core samples," I told her, picking one up and examining it. The flecks of mica embedded within flashed as I rotated it.

"Hundreds of them," she said, awed. "Watch your step, or you'll be sleeping with them. What was this place, Ian?"

"Part of a mining operation, I guess. They must have been drilling, looking for gold. Or silver. Or copper. Who knows?" I took off my backpack and tucked away a few cores as souvenirs.

Piper did, too. We were young and starry-eyed in those days. Her golden hair shone like the moon rising above a misty horizon, and I could always see the whole of the cosmos folded within her blue eyes. A foot taller than her, back then I had the build of a distance runner. We had no plans but to keep on keeping on, to live whatever could be lived. She rotated her final selection in her delicate fingers and said, "I know what this is, Ian."

"What's that?"

"A wish. I wonder if it ever came true." She slipped the core into her backpack and slung the pack into place.

On we walked. The track rose and fell and wound around. We came through a pass where an abandoned fire lookout crowned an adjoining peak. Needing no consultation, we scrambled up the broken slope to the metal tower and mounted the long stairs to the observation deck. The wood flooring creaked beneath our weight. Some of the planks had partially rotted out. Stepping carefully, we made a circuit of the outer platform, drinking up the view of the pine-swept slopes and valleys, then toured the inside. The place had a musky odor. A few grime-laden shelves and a deteriorated mattress were all we found. All other contents had been removed or decayed into dust.

I was ready to dismount, but "Once more around!" Piper insisted, so out and around we went. Puffy clouds floated overhead, almost close enough to touch. A hawk soared on the thermals this side of the next ridge east. To the north, we caught a glimpse of the track we'd been walking crossing a clearing. Farther on, it topped a low rise. There, something glinted in the sunlight.

Pointing, Piper cried, "Look! A fallen star!" And she was off, running down the metal stairs, hands gliding over the rails, boots clanging on the treads.

Laughing in her wake, I could barely keep up. "A cast-off sheet of tin, more like."

"You've no romance in your soul. Come on!"

We hit the ground and nearly vaulted from the mountainside. It was all we could do to keep our balance as we slipped and slid down the rock-strewn slope. "Then why do you follow me?"

"*I'm* not following *you*!" She caught my hand as we reached the track and pulled me northward, almost at a run. I supposed she was right, although I wouldn't have admitted it. She had sure snared me before I ever caught her, and if an adventure was to be had, she would be in the thick of it before I had worked out the route. So again, here we were, in hot pursuit of whatever had sparkled her eye. Not that I complained. She had a good eye for escapade.

But the way was longer than it looked from above. Eventually I had to slow her down. Breathing heavy, we walked hand in hand. We crossed that clearing as birdsong played in surround sound and came to the top of the rise. And there it was, Piper's fallen star, stationed incongruously a dozen paces off the trail.

A well.

A stone well with a small ridge roof, a crank, and a rope descending into the darkness, the whole looking like something conjured from a story book. On the lip of the well sat a sterling silver cup that gleamed in the sun as though the daystar had descended from the sky and filled it.

"What did I tell you?" Piper said. She laughed and led me by the hand to the well.

I puzzled over the structure. "What's *this* doing here?"

"Astute question," someone said, and we both started. Nobody was attached to the voice.

I had never seen Piper frightened, nor was she now. "Where are you?" she asked, her voice half wary, half glee.

"Where you seldom look," the voice replied. "I will make myself plain."

She wasn't plain. She was beautiful. Piper and I somehow parted without awareness of moving, and the interloper stepped between us. Her red hair hung in ringlets to her waist, splashing over her green dress, a dress embroidered with silver and edged in lace. She gazed into the depths of the well and ran her pale fingers over the cool stone lip.

I had lost my voice in astonishment, but Piper, for whom the world overflowed with magic by course, asked, "Who are you?"

"I'm variously known," the woman replied. "Some call me Caolainn."

Piper set her hand to the stone, too. "Is this yours?"

"Today it is for you." She looked at me, her eyes like a gathering storm. "For both of you." She took hold of the crank and turned.

The mechanism creaked as the rope wound onto the spindle. Shortly, a bucket filled with water rose from the depths. Caolainn lifted the silver cup and dipped it into the bucket. "If you wish. If you dare." She offered me the cup.

I didn't understand. "What's this for?"

Without answer, she turned and offered Piper the cup.

Piper took it and looked into the jostling liquid. "*I* know. It's a wish." She looked at me, eyes filled with wonderment. "This is a wishing well, Ian."

Caolainn neither confirmed nor denied.

Piper lifted the cup to her lips. After a moment's hesitation, she lowered it again without drinking and gave it back. With a solemn nod, Caolainn accepted it and turned to me, cup proffered.

I trusted neither my eyes nor my mind, but my heart was another matter. I knew with burning certainty what I wanted. I took the cup, drank, and gave it back. Caolainn set it on the well and stepped away, still silent, and when next we knew anything, Piper and I were on the dirt track, alone together, no well in sight, no sign of Piper's fallen star, only the mountains and the forest and us.

We neither spoke nor finished our hike. We had reached the end of the world. Where else could this path take us? So we about-faced, carried our core samples and our memories back to camp, and that night with an owl calling in the dark and Piper enfolded in my arms, her breath warm on my chest, I asked a question I feared might have no answer.

"Why didn't you drink?"

She clung to me all the tighter. "Why did you?"

"I don't know. I don't even believe in . . . whatever it was."

Time passed. I stroked her soft skin. Her muscles relaxed and her breathing slowed until I thought she slept, but no. "I couldn't wish for anything I don't already have."

That hardly sounded like Piper.

"Your turn," she prompted.

Somehow, I found enough courage to say it. "Because maybe someday the adventure grows cold. Because maybe someday you *won't* wish for me anymore."

She propped herself on her elbow, her face close to mine, a shadow in the dark. "You *are* the adventure, Ian. You *are* the adventure." Then she settled her head on my chest and listened to the beating of my heart. "But it's a good wish, just the same."

You know the old saying: "Be careful what you wish for. You might get it."

Sixty-two years our adventure lasted, not all of it spent running through the mountains. Not even most of it, truth be told. We worked jobs, raised a few children, nursed each other through sickness, propped each other up and pulled each other out of slumps. Sometimes I held her back, sometimes she weighed me down, but we couldn't part ways, whether for sake of the wish or from simple mule-headedness. And in sum it was good. We could have gone on forever, if not for one thing. We never saw the cancer coming. By the time it made its presence known, Piper had so little time left. We had so little time left.

"If you wish," Caolainn had said. "If you dare."

I had dared wish never to be parted from Piper. Now, with her body reposing in the earth, it seems my wish will be granted. I feel the encroaching dark. I diminish and know I soon must follow her into the night. For I only have heart for a world with her, an eternal world.

That could never have been this world.

I wish it still, that it may be another.

Orca

"That ain't real," Diamond Dan Ricci insisted.

Al Moretti, his right-hand man, shook his head. "Dunno, Mr. Ricci, but I'm not gonna poke it."

Ricci gave Moretti an annoyed look but didn't order him into the water. The huge black and white mass floating there looked all rubbery and fakey, or if not that then deadish. But it couldn't be dead because it couldn't ever have been alive. "It's a kiddie toy or something."

Moretti gave the boss an annoyed look of his own. "An eight foot kiddie toy?"

"I seen orcas," Ricci snapped.

"Where?"

"In the ocean, moron. From my yacht." Ricci pointed. "They ain't that small. Twice as big, at least. Maybe three times."

"So it's a baby."

Self-control not being his middle name, Ricci punched Moretti's arm. "Don't be stupid. What's a baby orca doing here?"

Moretti shook his head and shrugged, but it turned out he was right on one point. It wasn't a kiddie toy. The thing in the water moved, slowly twisting, slowly turning, slowly opening a toothy mouth and closing it again, forcing a spray of water into the air.

Ricci took a step back. "Schiavone."

Moretti looked ill. "Gotta be. Just his style. I'll tell the boys to keep a sharp eye out."

"Yeah," Ricci muttered. "You do that." And as his underling left to muster the troops, Diamond Dan adjusted his swim trunks and wondered how the hell Schiavone had gotten this thing into his basement swimming pool.

Mr. Smith's Shed

The golden light shimmering in Mr. Smith's back yard was all Robbie could see at night after he turned off his bedside lamp. Later, with his parents asleep, the house rested in silence save the whoosh of air pouring from the vents, cool in the summer, warm in the winter. But sometimes, in the dead hours after midnight, Robbie would wake to a quiet ringing, as though someone far away was forging a sword, folding and hammering, folding and hammering, and he would go to the window and look out at that golden light and wonder what Mr. Smith was up to. And then it would stop, and Robbie would return to bed and maybe dream of robots and warriors battling on a distant planet.

Robbie couldn't remember a time when that light wasn't there, shining like a conference of fireflies. He had just turned ten years old, a whole decade. As he got dressed the Saturday morning after his birthday, he decided a decade of mysterious lights and sounds begged for investigation. What could an old man possibly be up to, forging a sword in the night over the course of a decade?

At the breakfast table, Robbie poured his chocolate cereal and set the box before him, its back facing him to read as he ate. Dad hid behind his laptop, scanning the morning news and sipping black coffee. Mom passed by and tousled his sandy hair on her way out. "Showing a couple of houses this morning," she told the menfolk, who didn't acknowledge her. "I should be back by lunchtime."

Robbie crunched his cereal. The car growled in the garage and carried Mom off to work.

"Don't ever be a politician," Dad said, picking up his toast. "Liars and thieves, all."

"I want to be a detective," Robbie told him.

"Mmm." Dad munched his toast and clicked the mousepad.

"I'm going to investigate Mr. Smith first."

"Good a start as any."

Finishing his breakfast, Robbie took his dishes to the sink and rinsed them. "See you later, Dad."

"Lawyers." Dad clicked to the next story. "Don't be one of them, either."

Robbie spread his hands in frustration. "Detective, Dad. Detective."

"Mmm."

Robbie emerged from the house wearing his dark blue jacket, his hands shoved down in the pockets. The wind stirred his hair. He looked up at the ragged, gray clouds scuttling by, at the gold and red leaves twitching and dropping from the trees. A fine, mysterious day for sleuthing. From the sidewalk, he inspected the neighborhood, a ramshackle collection of modest houses built fifty or more years before. More decades than he'd been around, anyway. His house was the best, a two-story brick place that looked like a mansion compared to Mr. Smith's white, vinyl-sided Cape Cod.

Robbie paced the sidewalk in front of Mr. Smith's, sneaking glances in the windows, or trying to. The house guarded its secrets well. He saw nothing but reflections of trees, clouds, and himself. Returning, he studied the chain link fence surrounding his neighbor's yard, another defense to keep out the curious. Mr. Smith had no dog. He barely had any landscaping, for that matter, and only that big white shed in the back corner of the yard, the shed with the window through which the golden light poured every night. Clearly the fence was to protect that shed.

Robbie was proud of that deduction. But why would anyone guard a shed? It must be a hideout. Or a secret laboratory.

He turned and shuffled through the dew-laden grass on his side of the property line. Father had mowed recently, and the clippings clung to his shoes. His parents had no dog, either, nor any secrets requiring a fence. Their yard was honest and open. He put out a hand and let his fingers trip over the links as he brushed along Mr. Smith's fence, all the way to the back corner opposite the shed, where he stopped and checked the house. The back door was closed, but might Mr. Smith be watching through one of those windows that revealed nothing?

No, he told himself. Mr. Smith stays up all night. He must sleep all day. Like a vampire.

Another fine deduction. He chuckled to himself at the thought of Mr. Smith, old, bald Mr. Smith, with fangs protruding from his mouth. But that was silly. Mr. Smith probably had no teeth.

The shed's window, a great darkened eye, slumbered just above Robbie's head. Holding to the fence, he pushed up on his toes and tried to peer in, but it revealed no more than the house windows. He next checked the shed door. Padlocked.

Now what?

A real detective would get a warrant. If he had a warrant, he could knock on Mr. Smith's door, demand to be taken into the shed, and the old man would be forced to reveal his dark secrets. But Robbie didn't know where warrants came from or, really, what they even looked like. He toyed with writing his own warrant, but Mr. Smith would probably know it wasn't real. Adults could be clever like that.

Then Robbie got a better idea. He would wait for nightfall. Once Mr. Smith slipped into the shed, closed the door, and turned on that golden light, that window would reveal all.

Robbie's parents had company that night. Dad's old army buddy Sam brought his wife Carlie over for dinner, and long after Robbie was in bed the adults were still talking and laughing, effectively shutting down his investigation. Around midnight, an irritated Robbie went to the window, parted the curtains with his finger, and peered into the night through the narrow gap between the panels. The shed reposed in darkness. He watched for fifteen minutes, yawning, legs aching, and nearly gave up. But then a moving shadow caught his eye, Mr. Smith's back door inching open. A bent old form emerged and crossed slow and silent to the shed. It fumbled with something—the padlock, Robbie was sure—and then merged into the structure. A moment later, golden light flared in the shed's window, faintly illuminating the grass.

Try as he might, Robbie saw nothing through that window but light. The adults were still talking and laughing, so he returned to bed, pulled up the covers, and waited for the party to end.

He woke to a quiet ringing. Rubbing his eyes, he rolled over and checked the illuminated clock on his nightstand. Three sixteen. Kicking off the covers, Robbie went to the window and parted the curtains. The golden glow was still there, and the ringing floated in on the dark, over and over, metal striking metal, Mr. Smith forging a sword he would never finish.

Careful not to make a sound, Robbie dressed and crept from his room to the coat closet. He pulled on his winter coat, tied the hood, and with painful care unlocked the door.

Outside, stars twinkled in a clear, cold sky. Sirius, the eye of the great dog, blazed in the south next to his master, Orion. Robbie's father had taught him those stars last winter. They were his favorites. But duty called, so he slipped around the house and, making as little noise as possible, came to the fence by the shed's golden window. Steadying himself on the fence, he drew in a long, chill breath and raised himself up on his tiptoes.

He saw.

He saw old Mr. Smith, rocking in a rocking chair, covered with a blanket, a space heater glowing on a bench by his side.

He saw old Mr. Smith, rocking, an iron horseshoe in each hand, slowly banging them together. They rang like someone forging a sword.

Robbie watched, uncomprehending, until his toes hurt. And then, just before he lowered his feet back to Earth, Mr. Smith looked up, looked at the window, looked slack-jawed at Robbie.

The ringing stopped.

Robbie wanted to shrink down to the size of an ant. Not breathing, he crept along the fence toward the front of the house.

"Robbie? What are you doing out at this hour?"

Robbie froze, one hand on the frigid fence rail. Mr. Smith had opened the shed door. His frail form cast an inky shadow on the lawn. He'd caught Robbie spying. Without even a warrant.

"Good lord, boy. Hop the fence and come in here where it's warm."

He should have run, but somehow he couldn't. He swallowed and hopped the fence, hoping Mr. Smith wasn't a murderer. The old man slipped back inside the shed and sat in the rocker. Robbie followed, eyes darting every which way, trying to take in everything. There wasn't much to take in, just a shed with a few tools hanging on the wall, some old paint buckets, the bench, the rocking chair, the space heater, the horseshoes.

"Close the door," Mr. Smith commanded. "Keep the heat in."

Robbie closed the door and stared at the old man. He felt like his eyes were as wide as an owl's.

Mr. Smith adjusted his blanket and began to rock. "So what's the story? There must be a story."

A strange question. It wasn't Robbie's story. Robbie was only investigating. The story surely belonged to Mr. Smith?

"Noises in the night, I suppose." Mr. Smith picked up the horseshoes and clanked them together.

Robbie nodded.

"I used to play horseshoes." Clank. "You know how to play?" Clank.

"No," Robbie said, then added, "Sir." Being respectful just might save his life.

"Can't throw them anymore myself." Clank. "Used to, though, me and Marie." Clank. "That was before you were born. Before your folks were married, even." Clank.

Robbie thought that must have been more decades ago than he could count.

"She died." Mr. Smith sighed and set the horseshoes on the bench. "The sound brings her back." His eyes looked somewhere else, somewhere not inside the shed, maybe not even inside the world.

Robbie cleared his throat.

Mr. Smith's gaze returned to the here and now. "Go on, then. Ask."

This wasn't the mystery he expected. He had a hundred new questions, now. Where to begin? "Do you sit here all night?"

"All night."

"And sleep all day?"

"Yep."

"In the house."

"Yep."

Robbie shuffled his feet. "Why?"

Mr. Smith ran a finger over the horseshoes. "How old are you?"

"A whole decade." Robbie thought he'd tell people that from now on. It sounded more grown up than ten.

A little smile tugged at Mr. Smith's mouth. "All that, huh? Still, I'm not sure you're old enough to understand."

But now that Robbie knew there was nothing to fear, he found himself determined to finish the investigation. He puffed himself up. "Try me," he insisted.

Robbie slept late Sunday morning. So did his parents. Usually they would be up for church, but the adults had had a late night, too, even if not as late as Robbie's. It was nearly eleven before he was seated at the table with his cereal. His father was engrossed in his computer, his mother staring into her coffee and chatting on her cell phone.

"I finished the investigation," Robbie told Dad.

"Investigation?" Dad didn't look up.

"Of Mr. Smith."

"Who won?"

Robbie stirred his cereal, swirling the chocolate bits around in the milk.

Dad sipped his coffee.

"What's it like when someone you love dies?"

Dad peered over the top of the screen. He studied Robbie for a minute before returning to the news. "I don't know. Why do you ask?"

Robbie swirled his spoon through the bowl. "Just curious."

Another sip of coffee, another click of the mouse.

"Can we make a horseshoe pit?"

"Horseshoe pit?" Dad pushed his computer away and folded his arms on the table. "What got you interested in that?"

"Saw it online. Looks fun." Robbie shrugged.

"Sure, I guess. I've never played it, though."

Robbie spooned up cereal and held it aloft while milk dribbled back into the bowl and splashed onto the table. "I think Mr. Smith has," he said. "Maybe he can teach us."

An Incident at the Mall

Frazzled and late and dressed in blue, Melody slipped into the seat at the table in the mall's center atrium. "Moron!" she spat in a whisper as she plopped her blue saddlebag on the table.

Bernard stared first at her clothes and then the bag. "What the hell? I said change from blue to green."

"You said green to blue!"

"The guy is red-green colorblind! He's supposed to see you in blue!"

"And what's the deal with that door?"

Subject-changing always was Melody's best defense, Bernard grumbled. "What door?"

"You said go through the next door. The service corridors are back there. I got lost!"

Bernard shut his eyes. "I said go into the next store! Change in the dressing room in the next store!" She pointed a finger in argument, but he cut her off. "You at least got the stuff?"

"No!"

"What!"

"He didn't have any!"

"It's a jewelry store! How can he not have any?"

"Next time do your research better! They only sell *real* jewelry!"

Bernard nearly tore his hair out. "Not bling! Rings! Wedding rings!"

Melody snatched back her bag and slapped it into her lap. "He didn't even know what wedding bling was."

"How did you find your way out?" Bernard asked wearily. Melody and Bernard, he thought. Bonnie and Clyde, he thought. No contest, he thought.

"A security guard helped me."

"Oh, God." He looked around. Police were converging on their table.

"This," Melody said darkly, "is all *your* fault."

An Incident at the Grocery Store

"It should be here," Bernard muttered, pushing soda bottles around. The grocer's shelf was so tightly packed, he might have been working a sliding tile puzzle.

Melody watched impatiently. "You sure he said soda?"

"Yes." Hidden among the liquid sugar should be the drop, front money for a job they'd been hired to do. Center of the soda aisle, fourth shelf up.

"Maybe you misheard." Tired of waiting, Melody wandered off to look at the chips.

Irritated, he glanced back at her. "Hey! Keep watch!"

"Nobody's coming." She snagged a package and read the ingredients. "Maybe he said baking soda. God, look at the salt in this stuff!"

Why, Bernard wondered, did she warp everything like that? Soda it was. But fourth shelf up or down? He got on his knees to check. The shelves soon looked like a one-year-old had been playing among them. Head stuck halfway back, he heard a sharp rattle, then loud crunching. "What are you doing?" he snapped.

"These are terrible," Melody said around a mouthful of something.

Oh God, Bernard thought, *not again*. He extracted himself from the bottles and looked around, alarmed. Nobody there. Yet. He got to his feet and snatched the bag from her hands. "Cut that out!"

Melody gave him one of her dark looks, then gazed upward. He followed her eyes.

Security camera.

Rapid footfalls approached from around the end of the aisle.

She nodded at the bag. "Oh, Bernie," she said sadly. "You're in trouble again."

Happy New Year!

Dashing and debonair in his monkey suit, Bernard couldn't breathe. Should he exhale, the string quartet, every gowned and tuxedoed guest, even the glittering ballroom itself might blow away. Melody hung on his arm, laughing, clinking glasses with some rich camera-toting fool named Jack who grinned down her cleavage. Bernard wanted to punch his face.

Still, they were in. What could go wrong? His eye strayed to the solid gold porcupine adorning the banquet table, the Porcupine Yacht Club's legendary mascot.

"Ladies and gentlemen!" the master of ceremonies boomed. "Fifteen seconds to midnight!"

Cheers rose and lights fell. As the countdown began, all eyes turned to the smoldering stacks of the model ship centerpiece on the head table.

"Ten!" the throng shouted with joy. "Nine!"

At five full dark engulfed the room. Fireworks and smoke erupted from the ship, commanding attention, blinding everyone as Bernard slipped over to the porcupine. At "Happy New Year!" pandemonium reigned.

Bernard snatched the statue. A flash of light erupted from somewhere not the ship. He froze for an instant, then stashed the object in a prearranged hidey hole in the floor.

The lights went up. Once eyes adjusted, someone shrieked, "The porcupine! It's gone!"

A stunned silence fell, broken only when Jack snarled, "My camera's gone, too!"

Connecting the dots, Bernard's heart sank. *Oh God*, he thought.

Not again.

Melody tapped Jack on the shoulder and handed back his camera. "Oh," she said innocently, "was this yours?"

Washed Up

"Melody," Bernard whispered as the Mercedes stopped before the bath house. "Help!"

Melody stared ahead, miffed. "Help yourself."

He touched her shoulder. "You know I can't."

They sat locked into the back seat, his charcoal suit complementing her little black dress. At the wheel, Randolf Simmons, a spiffy fellow with slicked hair, parked in front of the bathhouse and killed the engine. "Return my diamonds," Simmons snarled. "Then we'll go inside and make your deaths look like a drowning accident."

Bernard cringed. He didn't know how he'd blown the job or why Melody had turned so belligerent. Granted, he shouldn't have insinuated this mess was her fault. She'd played her part perfectly for once. But God and life smiled on her, not him. She knew he couldn't extricate them. "An honest mistake, Mr, Simmons. We didn't know…"

"Shut up." Simmons stretched his palm towards Bernard. "Diamonds."

Unexpectedly, Melody pressed her nose to the window. "Wow! You have a whole bathhouse!"

Simmons blinked. "Sorry?"

"We just have a bath*room*, not a bath*house*. Do you have bed houses, living houses, and dining houses, too?"

Simmons retracted his hand. "Er."

"That's real wealth! You can't possibly need these little sparklies." Melody plucked the diamonds from Bernard's pocket and pushed them at Simmons. "But here you go. Like Bernie said, just a mistake." She leaned forward and whispered, "He's error prone, you know." Her breath ticked Simmons' ear. Pleasantly.

After a confused Simmons abandoned them in the car, forgetting his diamonds in his eagerness for a relaxing bath (or whatever), Bernard stroked Melody's hair. "Thanks, love. Forgive me?"

"You wish," Melody grumped.

Teleférico

What a view! Nat Sanderson leaned over the rail, face and arms dangling over a cliff that plummeted to the rippled sea. The bulk of a sheered-off mountain towered on his right, its red and gray strata spanning a thousand feet head to toe. Below, perched above a narrow beach, terraced fields undulated in rich soil washed from the heights over the millennia. The ocean stretched to the horizon beneath a mostly cloudless sky, its dark cast broken here and there by glints of sunlight.

A salt-laden breeze mussed Sanderson's light brown hair, carrying smells of seafoods and meats from the Restaurante Teleférico do Rancho. He stood on an observation deck perched atop a wide rock pillar adjoining the glass-walled eatery, soaking up the enormity of the world and envying the freedom of the sea birds wheeling above the waves. Fresh from lunch, he wore a light gray sports coat and dark gray cords but no tie.

It was a room temperature day. He removed the coat and slung it over his arm, then leaned over the glass-paneled railing once more to thrill in the drop. It consumed him. He felt he was floating, soaring with the birds, his fingertips brushing the volcanic wall as he swooped by. So lost was he in the sensation that he didn't notice the woman who stepped to his side and gazed down with him.

Not until she spoke words he couldn't understand.

Startled, Sanderson turned. Probably around forty-five, his own age, she was a petite woman with dark hair that danced about her shoulders in the breeze. Her burgundy dress, cinched at the waist with a thin black belt, fluttered at her knees. She gave him a little smile, a smile much like his wife Karen's. It planted his feet on solid ground again. Wistfully, he returned the smile. "I'm sorry, I don't speak Portuguese. Only English."

She laughed. "Naturally. American?"

"Iowa. Des Moines. Know where that is?"

She set a finger to her cheek and frowned in mock concentra-tion. "In the middle?"

His smile broadened. "Bingo."

"I imagine Iowa is nothing like this." She considered his face. "Your eyes give you away. You've fallen in love with Madeira, haven't you?"

Sanderson watched the ripples on the dark sea. "I've never seen anything like it. I came here for the cliffs, you know."

She watched with him. "How would I know that? We only just met."

"When you're right, you're right. Nat Sanderson." Sanderson ex-tended his hand to her.

"Mariana Couto." She took his hand in hers, her touch as light as air, not unlike Karen's. "So you like cliffs. Not looking for one to jump from, I hope?" She winked.

Sanderson nodded at the seagulls wheeling on the wind. "If I could flap my arms and fly like them, I would!"

"And I would watch and cheer."

That definitely wasn't like Karen. "Actually, I'm a cliff tourist. Yes, cliff tourism is a thing. We circle the world just to stand atop cliffs and drink down the adrenaline rush, basking in the awe and fear tin-gling through our bodies, head to toe and back again."

Mariana laughed. "You could save yourself the money and move to a clifftop."

"We don't have any in Iowa. The state is one long, slow slope from northwest to southeast. The ground crawls two hundred miles to drop as far as this mountain does in twenty feet."

"We do have houses, you know." She swept her arm toward the carpet of white buildings and burnt orange roofs spread along the coastal slopes.

"As I said, I don't speak Portuguese."

"I'll teach you." She winked. "Why not? We have this nice cliff to keep you happy."

"One cliff isn't enough. I'd still travel."

She shook her head, but with a sparkle in her eye that told him she savored his contrariness. "Why?"

Also not like Karen. Yet Mariana's height, her hair, her narrow face—she could have been Karen's cousin. "Because every cliff is different. I admit, this is the most spectacular view I've ever seen. I'll never forget it. But it's not, say, the Bunda Cliffs on the south coast of Australia."

"Can those be grander than ours?"

"Not as high, but over sixty miles long, with a thick, white sandstone layer near the base. The wall stretches horizon to horizon, a jagged line that looks like a giant took bites out of it. And in front of you, the Antarctic Ocean churning all the way to eternity. When you look out over that water, you feel like you're standing on the edge of the world."

She faked a great shiver. "Ooo, I don't think I'd like that. It sounds creepy!" They laughed together. "Do you do anything on your trips besides peer into oblivion?"

"Surprisingly little. I had lunch at the restaurant." He nodded at the unpretentious building perched on the edge of the cliff. Behind its glass walls, diners reveled in food, companionship, and the unparalleled view. "I enjoyed that."

"And your wife? Surely you have a wife?"

He winced, half at Karen's absence, half at Mariana's resemblance to her. "She stayed in Des Moines. Said she'd had enough of terrifying precipices. Said she was starting to think I planned on pushing her off one."

Mariana leaned over and whispered, "Was she right?" He gaped until she tossed her head and laughed.

Relieved, he smiled. "For a minute I thought you were serious."

"I've never been accused of that. So how can you afford to travel the world looking for terrifying precipices to not shove your wife over?"

Sanderson didn't care to talk business, not in a place like this that rendered human concerns so insignificant. "I have my own company. Nothing a woman like you would find exciting. Let's just say my liquid assets suffice to get me wherever I want to go."

"Mmm, I'll bet." She turned and leaned on the rail, suddenly melancholy. "I used to have money, too."

He didn't care to ask. He only wanted her good cheer back. He inhaled the warm air while the birds soared and the endless, undulating ocean drew his eyes to infinity. He willed her to get lost with him in its grandeur.

But she didn't. "It was my great idea, the Teleférico do Rancho."

Sanderson turned, surprised. "The restaurant?"

"Nooo." Mariana laughed. "The cable car system. The restaurant is named after it. See?" She pointed the other way to a covered platform from which massive cables descended along the face of the cliff. On the platform, an orange gondola waited for passengers. "Before I built it, the fields below could only be reached by boat. My grandfather farmed down there. I remember how hard it was for him to get produce back to the villages. He's gone now, but I remember. I built the teleférico to help other farmers. And sure, to make some money. I thought tourists would pay to ride it. Tourists like you." She grinned and poked his shoulder.

It sounded like a good plan to him. He would certainly pay to ride down the face of that cliff, to be suspended midair, dwarfed before its red and gray bands. "What went wrong?"

She shrugged. "Economics. It didn't pan out the way I expected. I put everything into building and maintaining the system and couldn't earn enough back. Now my money is almost gone. I may have to shut down."

Her sadness nearly smothered him. He nearly asked how much the teleférico cost to operate but stopped himself. *No business! I'm only here for the cliffs.*

"Hey." Her eyes brightened. "Would you like to ride it? Only ten Euros for the pair of us. "

"I'd love to." He pulled his jacket on.

"Come on!"

Mariana grabbed his hand and pulled him at a run to the platform. They were the only ones there, aside from the operator. Sanderson paid the fare. She nearly shoved him into the car and jumped into the seat beside him. The cabin could hold six passengers, so they had plenty of room, but she settled herself close, her thigh touching his. He hardly noticed. The car lurched and started down. He marveled at the expanse of dark basalt scarred by white dikes. Far below, a matching gondola began to trundle upward on its return trip.

They glided down the cables alongside the exposed history of the volcanic island. Mariana pointed and chattered about the green fields and gray beaches, offered statistics on the number of trips the cars made up and down each year and the tonnage of produce ferried up. Sanderson let the numbers float by like the clouds over the ocean. He reveled in the long, slow descent, dwarfed by mountain and sea. He felt like an ant forced to confront the majesty of the universe.

They debarked at the lower platform, and she grabbed his hand again. She walked him among the terraced fields and across the beach. She waded into the ocean, cupped her hand, scooped up water, and splashed it on him. He laughed with her and returned the favor. They gazed up at the mountain towering over them and the restaurant far above. Sanderson lost track of the time while they explored the shoreline and the base of the cliff until Marianna said they must go, before the cars stopped running for the night.

They rode the cables back to the heights with Sanderson counting strata most of the way.

"Worth ten Euros?" Mariana asked.

"Worth ten thousand!"

She laughed. "I'll take it."

"I'll give it to you."

She laughed again, but then saw the serious set of his face. "No, Nat. God, no! I'm joking."

He took her hand in his. "I'm not. I don't know what it costs to operate this thing, but I want you to keep it going. For the farmers. For the tourists. For the locals. For people like me."

She bit her lip. "What would your wife say?"

"Nothing. She lets me handle the finances, and anyway, we won't miss a nickel." Sanderson took a checkbook and pen from his inside jacket pocket and scrawled out numbers. "I told you, I have enough to go anywhere and do anything. I want you to have this." He ripped the check from the pad and handed it to her.

Pushing it back at him, Mariana said, "I can't, Nat. It's sweet of you, but I really can't."

The car came to a stop. "Yes, you can." He folded the check, placed it in her hand, and closed her fingers over it. Then he rose, opened the door, and helped her out. "I've had a wonderful time. And I'll be back someday. You know I will. Maybe we'll see each other again."

She blushed. "I hope so. Will your wife join us?"

He shook his head and grinned impishly. "I think I've lost my chance to push her over the edge."

Mariana laughed and slapped at his arm.

They parted company as the sun settled into the sea.

Not until three years later when Sanderson returned to Madeira, when he dined once more at the Restaurante Teleférico do Rancho, when he rode down to the shore alone and walked the beaches and returned to the top without once seeing Mariana Couto did he give it much thought. Only then did he ask around and realize how spectacularly she'd played him. The Teleférico do Rancho of course had not been her creation, of course had not been owned and operated by her, of course was not bankrupting her. Indeed, nobody had ever heard her name.

But hey, for a mere ten thousand dollars?

He'd have done it all over again.

Confession

"This is important, child."

Annette hated that word. She'd spent three decades impressing her capability upon people, her maturity, her intelligence. She had left childhood behind when most of her peers were running door to door yelling, "Trick or treat!" Her mother, of all people, should know that.

Mother's wrinkled hand lifted from the white sheet and gently pushed Annette's golden hair back from her face. Her old blue eyes met her daughter's matching middle-aged ones. "You hear me?"

"Of course." She twined her fingers with her mother's, forcing herself to smile in mock patience. "Only tell me quickly. They'll be here with your dinner any minute now."

Mother turned her head and coughed. "I feel myself slipping away. Like the edge of sleep, when you don't quite know what's real and what's a dream."

"Nonsense. You're just tired." For all her maturity, Annette had to admit that patience still challenged her. She had tired of her mother's games years before. This particular one, this brink-of-death charade, had run for three months now.

Mother didn't deny it, but she stared at the ceiling with a strange light in her eyes, like something up there beckoned and would not be denied. "You were only ten when your father died. Twelve when I remarried. Fifteen when *he* died. So much death, and you so young."

"I survived," Annette said, her voice hard. "Let's not dwell on the past."

"You father died of lung cancer. Smoked like a forest fire, he did, since he was a boy. On his deathbed, he confessed something."

Annette felt the blood leave her face. Her father lived in her memory as a kind, stern, funny man, a man who could grill a steak and fix a car, a man who taught his daughter baseball and ran races with her and helped her through math homework. A good man. A man worth remembering. "I don't need to hear this, mother," she snapped, her voice wavering. "Whatever it is, it doesn't matter."

Her mother's face turned slowly. Those blue eyes had a distant, vacant look. "Yes, child. It matters." She sighed. Her eyelids fluttered closed. "He was a good man, but even good men have secrets. Good women, too."

"I don't care."

"You see," her mother said as if she hadn't heard, "he knew something about someone. Something that he'd kept secret for eleven years."

She still didn't care to know, but Annette relaxed. If her father's secret had been someone else's misdeed, at least it couldn't reflect badly on him.

"He knew, but never let on, that another man made you."

Thought, emotion, feeling, everything drained away in that moment, as though she'd been struck unconscious with a blunt object. Yet she could see her mother's face, hear her breath, smell the antiseptic air. And then a lone thought crawled up from the dark recesses of her dysfunctional mind: *Then who the hell am I?*

"Strange," her mother whispered. "I thought he'd never find out, but he knew all along, said nothing, and raised you as if you were his own. And at the end, when he confessed he knew the truth, he said that after he was gone I should marry your real father. Yes, your stepfather, he was your *real* father. When he died in that crash, I thought I had died ten times over. I thought my sins had doomed me. You were the only thing keeping me on this Earth anymore."

Mother reached out and found Annette's hand. Her head slowly turned, her eyes searched, searched, and found her daughter's. "Can you forgive me?"

Her mouth dry, Annette nodded, mechanically, because it was expected. But thoughts of forgiveness hadn't formed. Even the need for them failed to register. "Why are you telling me this now?" She hoped she didn't sound hysterical. "Why not take the secret with you?"

Her mother smiled a weak, pathetic smile. "Because they both loved you so much. That's important. You should know it."

Annette remembered. Her stepfather—her real father—had tried so hard, and she had pushed him away. He had been an interloper, a replacement, a fake. Or so she had thought. How could she have known the truth? Thinking back, she thought he must have understood, even through his pain.

Mother's fingers brushed her cheek. "Oh, child. Don't cry."

She didn't know she had been, but mother's fingers came away wet.

"So much pain, but so much love. In a strange way, you've been fortunate."

Annette held her mother's hand until dinner arrived, but by then the old woman had drifted into a sleep from which she would never wake. Later that night when Annette finally left, she left heartbroken, yes, but embracing, too, the feeling that she was indeed blessed.

The Test

People don't just vanish. Oh, sure, someone might fade into the night, their scent dissipating on the wind until not even the most persistent bloodhound can sniff it out. Birds and mice may gobble up the breadcrumbs they dropped, leaving not even the most tenuous of trails. But solid bodies don't *vanish*. They walk into the sunset or fall off a cliff or are shot and dumped in the river. They may live or die, may return home or return to dust, but something always remains.

My brother Paul had not vanished. He had to be out there, somewhere.

His wife April called that late October morning, when cool air blowing in from the west had painted the trees in reds, yellows, and oranges and grocery store candy shelves lay bare, stripped of their wares in preparation for the flood of trick-or-treaters soon to wash over the sidewalks of our town. She called in barely controlled hysterics.

"Did he come to see you, Robert? Is he there now?"

"Why would he be here? You know we aren't on speaking terms."

"Then where could he be?"

I could hear her shoes tap the linoleum kitchen floor as she paced back and forth, back and forth. I could almost see her, petite April, golden-haired April, in that snug blue and green dress she so liked, the hem swishing about her knees, her hips swaying with each step, her cleavage peaking up at me. I flushed in embarrassment. I couldn't envision her without shame, not since Paul "caught" us. Our affair had been entirely in his head, but now it played out in mine, guilting me as surely as if I'd taken her into my bed. If I couldn't prove my innocence, it seemed, I could at least punish myself for it.

"How long has he been gone?" I asked.

She sniffed, and I heard a tissue being ripped from its box. "He left Saturday night after I fell asleep. I haven't heard from him since. No phone calls, no texts. He won't answer my calls."

I glanced at the calendar hanging above my particle board home office desk, although I knew well enough it was Monday. "Where did he go?"

"I don't know!"

"He didn't say?"

"I woke up at two thirty in the morning and he was gone, Robert. He was *gone*!"

Which wasn't at all like Paul. He could be quick-tempered, even rude sometimes, but not to April. I'd never heard him say a sharp word to her, not even that day when he thought the worst of us. He'd put that all on me. "Deep breaths, April. Let's think this through. Did you call the police?"

She whimpered. "I'm afraid to."

"Why?"

"What if they say he's been in an accident? Or he's dead?"

"Should I come over?"

The world held its breath. I'd made a dangerous offer. For so many reasons, she should say no. What if we tripped in the stress of the moment and fell into the infidelity Paul thought he had uncovered? What if he returned alive and well and found us together, even innocently together? In her silence, I heard her think, *Damn you, Robert, why did you ask?* Mortified, I willed the question into nonexistence, willed her to say no.

But she didn't.

"Please." So she whispered. And so I did.

April opened the door of their little white and blue bungalow as soon as I got out of my car. She stood back, hand on the doorknob, eyeing me as though I was the plumber come to fix a leaky faucet. The weakening autumn sun shone down, illuminating her hair, her face, her dark jeans and pale blue t-shirt. I hadn't seen her for nearly six years. If anything she had grown more beautiful, so beautiful I had to look away. I should never have suggested this.

Without a word, I passed through the door. She pushed it shut behind me. We didn't speak, didn't touch, didn't look each other in the eye. She led me to the kitchen and pulled out one of the beige padded chairs for me. A bit of stuffing dangled from a rip along the side. I sat and waited while she fumbled at the counter for cups and made coffee. I didn't want her to fuss over me. I only wanted her to sit with me, to draw comfort from my presence, but the ritual of serving a guest offered her a momentary respite from her fear.

Once the steaming cups were before us, she took the phone from the cradle and passed it to me. I called the police and reported Paul missing, then we settled in to wait. We half drained our cups in silence.

"Why did you come?" She stared into the dark liquid.

"You asked."

"You could have said no."

"We're family, April. Why wouldn't I have come?"

She peered harder into her cup. "You know why."

Why wouldn't she look at me? Why couldn't I look at her without guilt? I thought back to the day of our undoing. Paul, April, and myself prepping their living room for a coat of paint, she all joy and smiles, he running out to the garage to get more masking tape. She and I momentarily alone. A look passed between us, a foolish comment, a risque joke, another, a crescendo of laughter, a moment of embarrassment, then something else, maybe a momentary hug, maybe a peck on the cheek. She found her way into my arms and I into hers. But it wasn't like that. We'd just been horsing around.

Hadn't we?

Then the explosion. The shock. The anger and the fighting. And afterward, the guilt, the misplaced guilt. What had happened? Why had Paul not understood, not listened? What had we done to deserve his wrath?

But that was all a distant past I couldn't clearly see through the fog of emotions. I only knew the here and now. "For you," I told her. "Not for Paul. He doesn't— "

She looked up, eyes smoldering with anger and fear. "Stop."

Maybe I should have, but the betrayal had cut so deep. "*He's* the one who—"

"Just stop. He's a good man. Your brother. My husband."

"It hurts, April. Six years of agony."

She lifted her cup to her lips. I watched her drink. She didn't return my gaze.

Now I felt ashamed at hurting so much for so long. The injustice of that ate into me. Why should I bear the blame for everyone else's faults? "What did we do, April?"

She thunked the cup down on the table. "You know."

"A couple of stupid jokes. A bit of, I don't know. Nothing serious, anyway. Nothing real."

She finally looked me in the eyes, blank, uncomprehending, then laughed bitterly. "My God, Paul. My God."

I shrugged. It had to have been nothing serious. The alternative was too awful.

"You were all over me and I was all over you. You call that a joke?"

Had it gone that far? Had we meant it? In that moment, had we lusted for each other? Was that why I couldn't think of her without shame? I could imagine such betrayal, but I couldn't own it. That was something other people did, not me. Certainly not April. I had to protest. "I didn't do anything—"

"That I didn't want." She ran a hand through her golden hair. "It wouldn't have happened if he hadn't gone out to that damn garage. Not then. But another day? Maybe when we had you over for dinner and he went out to grill the steaks, or when you stopped by to pay back the money he loaned you and he wasn't there. Anytime the two of us were alone. I know you've paid dearly for it. So has Paul. Maybe it was inevitable. Maybe it's my fault. If so, I'm sorry."

I longed to hold her and comfort her, but I couldn't. Not in the flesh. So I closed my eyes and dared to embrace her in my thoughts. I could feel my arms encircle her, my hands trace the curve of her back, my body soak up the warmth of hers, our lips play over each other and our tongues caress and her breasts press hard against my chest. The memory was so vivid, I could no longer deny it. We had indeed done these things, just the once, just for a fleeting moment, but it had been real. Not by accident. By design.

"Hell."

She sipped her coffee. "Total hell."

"Okay. Look. What's done is done." Maybe it was, maybe it wasn't. It didn't matter anymore. We had betrayed Paul, and now he was gone. "I'm sure he still loves you. This can't be about that. Not after all this time." I said it, but I only believed the first part.

She looked up, blank, empty, as drained as her coffee cup. "I'm not sure of anything anymore."

An officer dropped by, asked questions, and took down answers. He informed us that Paul hadn't been admitted to any hospital in the area, hadn't been involved in any reported accident, hadn't shown up for work. April and I called family and friends. Nobody had seen him. He might have been a figment of our imagination. The day wore on until darkness crept over the world. As evening gave way to night, a gibbous moon rose and silence encroached.

"Will you be okay?"

She didn't answer. We were in the living room, April sprawled haphazardly on the sofa, I in a recliner not reclining. Eyes closed, face sagging with worry, she still looked beautiful. I remembered how she had felt in my arms and longed to feel her there once more.

"Should I . . ." I wanted to hear her say yes but feared to finish the question. *Just get up and leave*, I told myself.

She opened her eyes and stared at the ceiling. "Say it."

I swallowed.

"Say it, Robert. Please."

"Should I stay?"

Her eyes closed again. "Would you? If I said yes?"

If I did, Paul would never return. Somehow I knew that, as little sense as it made. The universe watched, breath held, waiting for us to falter, eager to pass judgement on us. It wanted us to doom ourselves, and him with us.

Suddenly angry, I told the universe to go to hell. I rose. "I'll call in the morning." I said it gently. The universe notwithstanding, I did care for her. That's why I had to leave.

Tears seeped from her closed eyes. "I'll be fine."

I doubted that. I doubted either of us would be ever again. But it was the only way. I left without saying goodbye.

I barely slept that night, and when I did, I dreamed of our past, of Paul stumbling into our passion, of him throwing me across the room, bloodying my nose, knocking the wind from me. In the dream, the beating didn't stop. It felt far worse than reality, yet somehow more tolerable, for I accepted that I deserved it and willingly submitted.

Morning came too late and too soon. I dragged myself out of bed, showered, made toast and coffee, called in sick. Work would could wait until my brother and my mind emerged from the void. Assuming they ever did. I resisted the temptation to call April but checked the clock again and again, wondering when or if she would reach out for me. That she didn't both worried and vexed me.

The day slipped from morning to afternoon before her call came. "Come see me," she said, and abruptly hung up. It was a minor miracle I didn't receive a ticket—or several—on the way over. Anticipation and nerves churning within me, I arrived to find Paul's black Ford Mustang parked in the driveway.

Sitting in my car, I stared at his. Within the house, he waited, thinking and plotting God knew what. I didn't know how I could face him, not after yesterday. Whatever abuse awaited me, I had no choice but to accept it should I step through that door. But April had called. She wanted me here.

Fighting off a rising tide of dread, I left my car and approached the door. Like yesterday, April was waiting and admitted me, her gaze never straying from the floor. And there was Paul, seated on the sofa, watching me with inscrutable eyes. He licked his lips but said nothing.

I had no desire to speak first, but the silence nearly buried us alive. Somebody had to say something. I shoved my hands in my pockets and tried to smile. "Glad to see you're okay. We were worried."

"Yeah," he admitted. "Sorry about that. Thanks for coming over."

I glanced at April, who acknowledged me with a shrug and motioned me to the recliner. She deposited herself next to her husband, who put an arm around her, tentatively, as though afraid of breaking her.

Again, the silence engulfed us. We couldn't look at each other. Once more, I was left to make the first move. "So what happened?"

Even I had trouble figuring Paul sometimes, but I could tell words were eluding him. I wouldn't have blamed him for accusing me all over, for questioning what April and I had done while he was gone, for throwing me out and warning me never to return. That might have been for the best.

"I couldn't live with it anymore."

If April knew what he meant, she didn't show it. A rabbit hiding in the tall grass, she kept perfectly still.

"With what?"

"Hating you. Doubting my wife. It was eating me up."

He had every reason to hate me and doubt her, but his method of facing it angered me. He'd done April, at least, a grave injustice. "So you ran off in the middle of the night? What the hell kind of response is that?"

"I didn't run away. I removed myself from the picture. To test . . ." He sighed miserably and pulled April close. She leaned into him, compliant if not happy.

My fingernails dug into the arms of the chair. Even if I deserved to be set up to fail, how could he have treated April so? If she hadn't been right there, I might have slugged him for that.

"I pushed it off the cliff, let it fly or fall as it would. That way I'd have no choice. I'd be forced to trust you. Both of you."

It took a moment for that to sink in. He hadn't tested us, but himself. I scolded myself for doubting him. April looked away, as embarrassed as I. I scrutinized her face and wondered how we had all come to this pathetic moment. Paul stared at the walls, out the window, anywhere but at us, as though his test hadn't ended. Maybe it never would. Which begged a question.

"What if you can't?"

"I can." He squeezed April and smiled at her, then nodded at me. "I know I can."

April turned to him and buried her face in his shoulder, simultaneously laughing and crying. "You're such an idiot," she told him. But for what? Testing himself? Trusting us? She didn't say.

"Guilty."

She might have been right, but I couldn't let it hang there. He hadn't seen us the previous day, hadn't heard us, couldn't possibly know what was really in our hearts, buried under a veneer of denial. So I had to insist, for my own sanity if not for his. "But what if you can't?"

April held her breath, and I could tell by the question in her eyes that she had to know, too. So I tried to explain. "While you were gone—"

He put up a hand to stop me. "I can. I will. This isn't yesterday, Robert, and it's not six years ago. It's today."

Which didn't make the past vanish any more than he had, nor could we be sure it would never return. Looking into April's eyes, I knew she felt the same. His certainty didn't change our frailty.

Still, Paul was right about one thing. Today at least offered a moment to make a new start. And maybe that would be enough. Because really, it's the only moment we ever have.

The Mountains in Morning

"They trick you. Draw you off your guard."

Park Ranger Jared Masterson raised his binoculars and scanned the undulating land. "What does?"

His partner Tess White breathed in the cool air and released it slowly. "The mountains."

Masterson studied the steep, rocky slopes and the mist pouring through the pass and spilling down ravines. That mist concealed scores of dangers from precipices to bears. Rescue situations arose all too often out here, but this wasn't one of them. A mystery confronted them now.

Tess came to his side. "This place especially. Don't you think?"

He hazarded a glance at her. She belonged here, with that raven hair and those smoky eyes as beautiful as a twilight sky. She could lower his guard further than any distraction nature might dish up. *Keep it professional*, he reminded himself. He took up the binoculars again. "Maybe. But something more is at work here. Seven experienced hikers fall to their deaths in one month, all along this stretch of trail? It doesn't make sense."

"Come on, Jared. Look at this place. Have you ever seen anything more beautiful?" She spread out her arms as if to embrace the land, then hugged herself, her face a study in bliss. "The rock, the forest, the broken sky. And that fog, like a feather-soft burial shroud wrapping the valley." She closed her eyes and inhaled, face tilted sunward. "Mmm, don't you just *love* the mountains in morning?"

Her enthusiasm seduced him. Jared watched enraptured as she reveled in nature's caress. He couldn't look away, for yes, he had indeed seen something more beautiful, standing right beside him.

Tess opened her eyes and favored him with a coy smile.

Jared swallowed, turned away, and scrutinized the rocky ground beneath his feet. This was a bad place for distraction. Half a yard off, the land tipped into a five hundred foot drop boiling with cloud. "Morning? It's two in the afternoon."

She sidled up to him and set a delicate hand on his shoulder. "Who cares about the time?"

He inched away to free himself from her touch.

"Don't pretend, Jared. You're no good at it." She closed in again, ran a finger down his arm and across his chest.

He took her hand in his to stop her. "Are you saying…you really want… "

He couldn't finish, but she understood. "You can't tell?"

He looked into her eyes and saw the answer. "But our work."

"Look where we are, Jared. It's so perfect. Work will wait."

Jared couldn't look at anything but her. She was more perfection than he could absorb. Yet as much as he wanted her, he couldn't. People had died here. He had to understand why before fate claimed another victim. He shook his head and gently pushed her back.

Tess sighed. "All business, aren't you? Fine." She scuffled to the rock ledge and peered into the depths. "So what do you think happened?"

He studied the ground here, there, before, behind. It neither revealed nor hid anything. "I don't know. Every incident took place in good weather. The ground doesn't look that treacherous, so probably not a simple misstep. Chased off the edge by a bear? Once maybe, but not seven times." He turned and found Tess inches away again, still smiling with hope.

"Distracted, maybe?" she suggested.

"By what?" He tried to back away, but she slipped her arms around his waist.

"Natural beauty?"

Jared nudged her off again and backed another step, checking with a glance his distance from the drop. If he wasn't careful, he'd journey into oblivion himself.

"Okay," she said. "I have a theory." She closed on him, voice whispering like a summer breeze in his ears. "Over there." She pointed across the void to the next ridge.

He looked but saw nothing strange, nothing that explained anything.

Her lips brushed his cheek. "Don't you see?"

He didn't, of course he didn't, because nothing was there. Just an expanse of air, the fog below, the ridge across the way. It occurred to him that Tess wasn't quite right in the head today.

"Let me show you."

Her fist slammed into his gut and knocked the wind from him. As he doubled over, she shoved him toward the brink. His arms flew wide, grappling for balance. His feet stepped into empty space and he plummeted, silent, into the soft embrace of the mist.

Tess watched him vanish in the gray, her eyes sparkling, her lips parted in awe, her breath caught in her throat. *Jared*, she thought, *you're cloaked in cloud!* She sank to her knees and wiped away a tear. "So beautiful. So, so beautiful. Can you see it, Jared? Can you see it *now*?" She inhaled long and deep, eyes closed, willing the gentle fog to envelope her body and lift her, carry her through the pass, up, up, higher than the peaks. She felt herself drift away on the clouds. "Yes," she breathed. "Oh my, *yes*! Don't you just *love* the mountains in mourning?"

In the Butcher Shop

When he stepped up to the butcher's counter, Jimmy Borden's face wore the look of a man who'd just seen another man killed: skin as gray as a foggy morning, eyes as empty as the hollows in a dead tree, the small list neatly written out by his wife twitching in his shaking hands. He should have taken a number, but he didn't and didn't have to. As the other customers became aware of his presence, they each took a step back, gaped, forgot their orders and their places in line.

"Good God, Jimmy," observed the butcher Tom Ashton in his usual offhand way. He placed his chunky hands, fingers spread wide, on top of the display case where beef and veal and pork and chicken and turkey in every cut had been arranged with military precision. His apron was streaked with red, but otherwise he was an immaculate giant, six and a half feet tall, his white paper hat settled just right on his head, his hands freshly gloved. "What happened, a car fall off the lift?" He smiled to show he was joking. Jimmy ran an auto repair shop on the other side of their tiny town, the only one in town, in fact.

Jimmy looked at him and shook his head. "Don't go there," he said in a weak, shaking voice.

Tom squinted at him, then returned to the job he'd been doing, packing up four t-bone steaks. "Don't go where?"

"Just don't."

"Hard to avoid a place you won't name."

"None of you should ever go there again."

Tom tried a different tactic. "I see you've got a list. Want to take a number?"

"What?"

"Take a number. Do something normal. Might calm you down."

Jimmy took a number, mechanically. He didn't look at it. "I

would never have thought it of him. Never in a million billion years."

A petite woman with hair dyed red and blue touched him on the arm. "Who?"

"Doc Meyer." He tried to swallow, but his throat was dry. "Old Doc Meyer."

"The veterinarian?" the woman asked. "What's he done?"

Jimmy shook his head. "You don't want to know. Just don't go there."

"Half the town goes there, Jimmy," a rotund old man told him. Anthony Masterson his name was, and he lived two doors down from Jimmy Borden. Most everyone waiting at Tom Ashton's meat counter knew Jimmy, and each other. The town wasn't all that big, after all, only a hair more than four hundred souls, and yes, with only two veterinarians in this end of the county, half of them probably did take their pets to old Doc Meyer.

"Not anymore," Jimmy said. "Not after this. It's Doctor Flannigan for me from now on. And for you, too, if you know what's right."

Tom rolled his eyes and shook his head. The other customers followed suit.

Jimmy covered his face with his hands, crunching the list. "The air smells like blood," he said to nobody.

"It's a butcher shop," Tom Ashton explained. Logic was his forte, it seemed.

"I'd never go to Flannigan," said a tall brunette lady with two young children, a boy and a girl, clinging to her hands. "He charges and arm and a leg." The children stared at Jimmy wide-eyed, waiting for him to catch up to their mother's economic analysis.

"Money!" Jimmy spat. "The root of all evil! Don't listen to it, not when this is going on!"

"So what," Tom said rather than asked, "is going on."

For the first time, Jimmy noticed the other customers. He drew a breath and smoothed his hair and unrumpled his wife's list. Then he silently read the list before answering, "I'd rather not say. There are children present."

The mother pulled her children close.

Anthony Masterson looked him in the eye. "Doc Meyer treats my dogs. He's good at it, plus close and reasonably priced. Why should I stop going to him?"

Jimmy leaned a hand on the meat counter. "He kills," he said.

"Kill?" Anthony asked. "Kills what?"

"Animals, of course. His patients."

Tom tugged at his ear. "Sure, he puts down animals that can't be saved. Every vet does that."

"I mean, he kills healthy animals."

"Ridiculous."

"I saw it, Tom." Jimmy straightened. He reread his list as though it had the power to banish his horror. "I saw it."

"So who's next?" Tom looked around. "Number thirty-four, looks like." But nobody raised a hand or a number or even looked at him. Jimmy's ghostly face commanded all attention.

"You know Claire Ferguson. Little old lady, lives alone with six cats, one nineteen with two paws over death's threshold, one fifteen with a questionable ticker, one a kitten, and three in between."

All murmured acknowledgements.

"The cat with the heart condition checked in today and didn't check out. Doc Meyer said the medicine just wasn't working anymore and the poor guy should be put down so he didn't suffer. Claire told me as I was coming in and she was leaving. She was heartbroken."

"Tough break," Anthony said. "But it happens."

"Sure, only Doc hadn't put the cat down."

Tom arched an eyebrow. "And you know this how?" He scanned his customers and asked, "And who's got number thirty-four? I know somebody here does." The tall brunette with the children raised her ticket and moved to the counter, her eyes darting between Tom and Jimmy. "Good afternoon, Mrs. Howell, what can I get for you?"

Jimmy regard Mrs. Howell and then her children and then the

steaks lying in the cool behind the glass. "I took my Pointer Sherlock in for an exam. Afterwards, back in the car, I realized I'd left my hat in the exam room, so I went in to get it. The back door was open, and I could see Doc in the surgery. The cat was on a table, still alive, and Doc was telling his tech . . ."

Jimmy leaned on the counter again and shook his head. His audience waited breathlessly.

"He was stroking that cat and it was purring and he was telling the tech, 'Vaughn Labs wants the brain and ChemCorp wants the liver and Five Star wants the kidneys.'"

Rolling his eyes, the butcher asked, "Mrs. Howell?"

"Oh." Mrs. Howell, still holding her children close, tore her eyes from Jimmy and looked at the meat. "Three pounds of boneless chicken breast."

"I'm sure the cat was done for anyway," Tom said as he packed the order.

Jimmy drew a long breath. "No, it wasn't. No more than you or I or any other living thing, anyway."

The woman with the red and blue hair raised her hand as though she were in a classroom. "How do you know it wasn't?" she asked, her voice as timid as a light breeze.

"Doc saw me. He stared at me like I was pointing a gun at him. Then he waved the tech away and came into the exam room. At first he couldn't find his voice. Then he asked why I'd come back, and I said I'd forgotten my hat, and he said okay and by the way whatever I'd heard wasn't what it sounded like."

"Probably wasn't," Anthony Masterson opined, then went to the counter to examine the wares.

Ignoring or not having heard the remark, Jimmy continued, "It was something, all right. I knew it was. He had that scared look a kid gets when caught stealing candy. I didn't say anything. I didn't know what to say or think. He babbled about the economy and how hard it was to pay people and buy equipment, and how he wasn't going to chisel customers like Flannigan does. I asked him what that had to do with cutting up animals. Oh, he said, labs pay for research materials. It's common practice, and the animals are dying anyway, so what's the harm? So I said what about that cat, was it dying? Yeah, sure, he said, in a few years. Besides, Claire Ferguson couldn't afford those heart meds, anyway."

Jimmy looked around for agreement, acknowledgement, sympathy, anything at all, but saw none, only dismissal and annoyance. "Don't you get it? There was no reason to kill that cat! None! Is there a chair here?"

There wasn't, so he sat on the floor.

"One cat," Mrs. Howell said as Tom Ashton handed her bagged-up chicken parts to her. "So what?"

"Not just one cat. He spilled it all out, like making a confession, only he wasn't sorry, just scared I wouldn't understand." He shuddered. "Understand! He does this all the time, kills animals he could treat instead, cuts them up, sells their organs." He looked around. "It could be your dog," he said, pointing at Mrs. Howell. "Or your cat." He pointed at the woman with the multicolored hair. "Or your parakeet." He pointed at Anthony.

"I don't have a parakeet," Anthony said. "I think I'm next, Tom. Number thirty-five."

"That's right," Tom replied. "What can I get for you?"

"I need some New York strip steaks. Five—no, make it six."

"I don't know," Jimmy said, reading his list for the third time. "Maybe he doesn't see the wrong he's doing, but if so he's blind. He lies to customers, tells them their pets need to be put down when they don't, just to make some extra cash. Isn't that wrong?"

Tom rapped on the countertop. "Jimmy, look at me. I sell cut up animals, right? You come in here to buy what I sell, right? Then you go home and eat it."

Looking over his shoulder from his seat on the floor, Jimmy snapped, "That's different."

"Why?"

"For one, these animals were raised for eating."

Tom shrugged. "Either way, we're not talking about human beings."

"And anyway," Anthony added, "Doc Meyer is right. Flannigan is a chiseler. You'd have to go thirty miles to Stevensville to find a vet as reasonable as Doc Meyer."

"What does that matter? Thirty miles, a hundred miles. You can't do business with a man who butchers animals for money!"

"You do business with me," Tom said.

Jimmy scrambled to his feet, livid. "Damn it Tom, that's not the same, and you know it!"

Mrs. Howell wagged a finger at him. "You're one to talk, Jimmy Borden. You ran over that squirrel earlier this summer. Remember that? How dare you complain about a good man like Doc Meyer when you're just as guilty?"

Jimmy gaped at her. He gaped at her children. He gaped at everyone.

Less timid than before, the woman with the multicolored hair said, "You sound like you want to put him out of business."

"You bet I do!" Jimmy told her.

"You must hate animals! Trying to put a vet out of business! My God!" She turned away in disgust.

A bewildered tourist stranded in an alien country, Jimmy gaped. "What is the matter with you people?"

Tom Ashton pulled off his gloves and snapped a fresh pair over his hands. Keeping his eye on his fingers, he said, "I don't think I'll be serving you today, Jimmy."

"What?"

"In fact, I don't think I want you in my shop."

"Yeah," Anthony Masterson agreed. "I don't think I'll bring my car to your shop anymore, either."

The others scrambled to join him, and Mrs. Howell upped the

stakes. "I'll tell all my friends not to take their cars to you, either!"

Stunned, Jimmy backed toward the door. "You can't be serious! Doc Meyer is . . . what he's doing is . . ."

Drawn up in a self-righteous rage, the woman with the multicolored hair pointed a sharp-nailed finger at Jimmy Borden. "You disgust me," she snarled. "Get the hell out of here. Get the hell out of town!"

Had there been stones on the floor, they might have stoned him. So he left, as pale as when he'd arrived.

He didn't know what he would do after that, what he would tell his wife, how they would even live from that moment on. Maybe they would leave town, after all.

But when the world's gone mad, where really can you go?

Driftwood

They kicked along the beach, sand flying before their feet, Richard and Randi, mirror images, male and female, dark hair rustling in the salt breeze, gull screeches in their ears, nostrils brimming with the dark scent of marine life, shadows swimming through their almost-old brains.

"Dad always liked you more than me." Richard kicked extra hard. A galaxy of sand grains spun before them.

Randi smiled a honey-sweet smile. "I'm the girl."

"And I'm the disappointment."

"The thief," she agreed. "The embezzler."

Richard's mouth knotted up. He tugged at the hem of his pale blue t-shirt and hiked up his white Bermudas. "I beat the rap, didn't I?"

Randi matched in her short white skirt and pale blue tank top. They hadn't consciously coordinated. No need. They possessed a natural harmony. Her laugh echoed the playful rush of waves. "Your lawyer double-talked the jury into a stupor."

"And so doing drained my life's savings."

"Money, money, money. You're here now with me." She leaned her head momentarily on his shoulder.

He kissed her hair. "Yet even you won't believe me."

Randi straightened and tugged at his arm as she had done when they were kids. "So what? I think you're brilliant, pulling off a stunt like that, walking away without a scratch."

"I'm covered in claw marks, sis. You're the only one who never mauled me or tried to make a meal of me."

"Well, of course. You're me and I'm you. Anyway, it doesn't matter. Dad's gone, heart stopped mid-beat, eyes glazed over, the mirror set to his lips showing not a trace of fog."

"Leaving you everything and me nothing." Richard stopped and swept the beach with narrowed eyes. He lingered over a snag of decaying red-brown driftwood nestled in the sand, working its way into or out of the earth. An apt metaphor for his life, he thought. "When did he change his will, anyway?"

Randi's eyes followed his and saw the world as he did, a crumbling realm where every brilliance was illusion, every glory a lie. "Does it matter? It is what it is."

But he insisted. "Before the verdict, or after?"

She sighed. "When do you think?"

"Probably as soon as the allegations popped up on his smart phone." Richard laughed, bitter. "One hint was enough, I'm sure."

Giving him a twisted smile, Randi punched him in the arm, lightly. "See? You didn't have to ask. No faith was ever lost between you."

He shoved his hands in his pockets. "Randi. It's not that. The money really is gone. All of it. Months ago, Dad took away the trust fund he'd set up for me. Now I'm penniless and days from homeless."

"Why didn't you come to me before?"

"I assumed he'd changed your fund terms, too. He knew your loyalties and would have taken countermeasures."

Randi tugged his arm again. "You worry too much. Come on!" She ran, pulling him to the driftwood snag. She poked at it with her toes. "You never know what's hiding under this stuff. Remember how as kids we turned over rocks to watch the bugs scramble? What do you suppose is underneath this?" She nudged a piece of it away. A hermit crab scrambled out of the tangle and skittered across the sand. She watched it go, breath held, eyes sparkling.

Richard watched, too, and felt her wonderment. "Can you help me now?"

"I'm almost insulted. You know I won't see you homeless."

The crab vanished in the distant sand and sun. "Yes. Sorry. Everything hit at once. The trial, the disinheritance, all that money turning to smoke and wafting up the chimney. And I honestly didn't think dad gave you options."

"He didn't, but that was before. He's no longer a god. Now *I* hold his whole universe in *my* palm. Come live with me for a few months. I'll fix everything."

Richard nudged the driftwood, curious to see what else might lurk below. "Strange."

"What?"

"If dad had lived . . ." He watched a few insects ramble over the decaying wood. "Impeccable timing. His death, I mean."

"Yes," Randi agreed. She tugged at him again and smiled a sly, sweet smile. "But why should that be strange?"

Falling

The vines hit him in the face. Over and over, no matter which way he turned or which way he stepped, no matter how careful he was, they slapped and stung him with the tiny green needles littering their surface, fine needles that pierced without pain and clung when he pulled back, igniting a fire in his skin.

I'm trapped in a cage, he thought, *a living cage holding me for some foul creature's lunch!* Sweat beaded on his forehead, neck, and arms. He squinted upward at the fractured rays of the sun, slender arrows of light raining down through the distant canopy, searing everything with their heat. Steam rose from the moist earth below his feet, filling the air with smells of green, damp, and decay. He choked on them.

No way out. I'm going to die here.

More frightening still, he didn't know where here was, much less how he'd gotten there. A mental void separated him from where he had been. He could remember the Turkmenistan plateau, the excavation, the strange bones the team had uncovered, the exhilaration thrilling everyone. A long, lean giant with curved spines on the tail, the strange fossil had great serrated teeth, grasping hands and four-toed feet. They'd never seen anything like it.

He remembered, too, the explosion, the roar of crumbling rock, ground disintegrating beneath his feet. His colleagues' screams echoed in his ear. The smell of the baked earth filled his nostrils as a great blackness swallowed him whole.

And then?

Nothing. The stately rotation of the universe. The passage of an age. His bones disarticulated, polished, and reassembled. He had been killed young and reborn old, his memory at once full and empty, all he had known erased, all he had never known filling him to overflowing.

And now here he was.

What the hell happened to me?

Pain exploded in his shoulder as a vine swayed into him. Wincing, he took the sting. He had to get out of here. Tentatively, holding his breath against the pain, he touched the thick tendril before him and nudged it. Beyond, he could see nothing but an impassable sea of vine

"Morrow! Is that you?"

The cry had come from above. Looking up, he found a great white branch meandering a couple dozen feet over his head. The vines dangled from the underside of that branch as well as others, but through a gap he could see, spread-eagled across the limb, a dark figure. Whoever it was waved an arm.

"Morrow! It's me, Farnham! Where the hell are we?"

He didn't know. He couldn't even be sure it really was his fellow grad student. This whole thing might be nightmare or hallucination. He stared dumbly at the shadow on the limb, trying to make out features.

"What's the matter with you, Morrow? Say something!"

It sounded like Farnham, all right. "I'm trapped," he called up. "These vines. They're covered in thorns. And I don't any more know where the hell we are than you."

"Should I come down?"

"No! There's no way out of here."

"Then you'd better come up."

Farnham was nuts. How could Morrow get up there?

"Climb, moron! Grab a vine and climb!"

Morrow didn't think he was the moron. He'd just told Farnham about the thorns, hadn't he? But what choice did he have? He could climb or die. Gritting his teeth, he laid hold of a vine, pulled himself up, and wrapped his legs around it. A million tiny explosions wracked his body. He turned his eyes heavenward and climbed, focused on the dark shape on the limb above. With each movement, pain coursed through him. He ignored it and put one hand over the other, pushed with his legs, inched upward with thorns biting him like a swarm of ravenous mosquitoes.

A few minutes or hours or years later, he reached the branch, hauled himself onto it, and collapsed, exhausted, with his back against the pale trunk.

"Out of shape," Farnham laughed.

Panting, Morrow couldn't spare energy for a comeback.

Farnham looked down at the damp forest floor. "So what do we do now?"

Morrow studied the canopy. Dark leaves shaped like hearts and spear tips encircled them, here and there pierced by splinters of light. Those damned vines filled the space below, all the way to the ground, all over the place. It was like no jungle he'd ever read about. How could they have fallen through a hole in Turkmenistan and landed *here*?

"Don't know. What do you think?"

Farnham grinned and shook his head. "Brains are your department. They just brought me for muscle."

Morrow closed his eyes. His beefy companion's self-assessment was probably better than he realized. The man had more affinity for football than paleontology. Still, he'd struggled most of the way to a Ph.D., so he couldn't be a complete idiot. Morrow was more studious, less the athlete, yet fit enough for field work. "Maybe," he suggested, "we can traverse the branches until we find a clearing."

"Dream on." Farnham carefully rose and bounced a little, arms outstretched for balance. The limb bounced with him. "Sturdy enough right here, but not out there. He pointed, then lowered himself again and looked up at the sky. "The rest of the crew must be up there. They'll figure out where we are."

"There's nothing up there but sky." Morrow couldn't fathom it, but certainly they weren't down a hole in the ground.

As Farnham turned to reply, the tree reverberated as though struck by lightning. The men scrambled for handholds as it shook again, again, again. "Earthquake," Farnham gasped.

Morrow doubted it. The vibrations came too far apart. The tree wasn't being shaken. It was being struck. His fingers dug into crevasses in the bark. Below, the vines whipped aside, and a *thing* came into view.

Farnham caught sight of it and threw himself down on the branch, legs extended along it, arms gripping its sides. "Don't move!" he gasped.

It might have been a dinosaur walking off a movie screen, but it was longer, leaner, with scimitar spines on its whip-thin tail and serrated teeth protruding from its upper jaw. Walking on two legs with its body horizontal, its arms tucked close to its body, it stood twelve feet high, half as high as the branch where the men perched. Its keen eyes took in everything as it pushed its way through the vines whose barbs couldn't puncture the animal's thick hide. It paused and sniffed, nose slowly tilting upward, then its eyes fixed on the spot where Farnham hid.

The creature turned, raised up, and wrapped its hands about the tree. Stretching its neck, it sniffed again. Morrow felt the air swirl about his face, smelled the hot, sour breath waft by. This animal, he realized, could have been brother to the fossil they had uncovered at the excavation. It stretched its forearm and tried to reach the branch, but its grasp fell two feet short.

Morrow looked to Farnham, still laid out on the branch, sweat dripping from his face onto the bark. He heard the creature's claws scrape the tree trunk. The whole tree shuddered.

"It's climbing!" Farnham whispered.

A single claw slid up the side of the branch by Morrow's feet. He pulled back but had no place to retreat. Looking up, he noticed the stub of a broken branch just above his head and another, thinner branch above that to his left. He took hold of the stub and hauled himself upward until he could grasp the higher limb. He barely had the strength to raise himself up, but somehow he managed, and the branch took his weight. Exhausted, he clung to it and looked down.

The beast hadn't given up. One hand draped over the lower

branch, feet scrabbling against the trunk, it forced itself higher. The tree shook under its efforts. Farnham hadn't moved. Fused to the branch, eyes closed, he buried his face in the bark.

"Farnham!" Morrow called, but the other didn't respond.

The animal got both its arms around the branch and worked its way outward, its feet still scraping upward along the trunk. Its hands had nearly reached Farnham's position when in a swift motion it pushed off from the trunk and wrapped legs and tail around the branch.

Death mere inches from him, Farnham finally moved. He scooted back, pushed himself up, and crawled outward, feet first. The creature continued its slow, inexorable advance, forcing its prey onto thinner and thinner wood. The branch bent and groaned beneath its weight. Morrow could do nothing but watch.

Wood snapped and splintered. Farnham lunged, flew through the air, and groped for a nearby branch as the animal fell with a piercing scream to crash on the forest floor. But the wood Farnham caught couldn't take his weight. It broke, and he, too, vanished into the vines. The only sound he made was a gasp, then silence filled the jungle.

Morrow leaned forward, hand outstretched as though he might yet catch Farnham and pull him to safety. He couldn't find his voice, could barely breathe, and dared not call out. He heard nothing, saw nothing but leaves and branches and vines, and through it all the fractured sunlight beating down, searing him.

Farnham never called or cried out, and Morrow never did climb down. He couldn't. Later when the sun dropped from the sky and darkness spun its web over this world, wherever it was, whatever it was, he pondered how strange this had been. Strange that this creature's brother had fallen into their world and perished a hundred million years past, and now here they were, having fallen into its world. Farnham was dead, Morrow soon to die. A hundred million years hence, would paleontologists here gaze in wonder on their bones? Would one of those people fall into Morrow's world? How many times had it happened, back and forth, over the ages? How had the worlds changed because of it?

He leaned against the pale bark and closed his eyes, spent to the point of death. Soon he would sleep. He didn't expect to wake in either world. He would die of exhaustion or grief or be eaten by a predator in the night.

But he might still wake in yet another world. He hoped so, and he wondered what that would be like.

Forest of Giants
(Indies Unlimited flash fiction editor's choice winner)

"Look!" little Samuel cried, bouncing on his toes. "Giants!"

Mom and Dad gazed up into the forest canopy. Dad nodded sagely while mom, smiling, patted Samuel on his three-year-old head. "That's right!" dad agreed. "Tallest trees in the world, redwoods. Why, some are over three hundred fifty feet tall!"

"Giants!" Samuel poked at the sky "Giants!"

Mom laughed. "Giants, and old folks, too. Some of them are over seven hundred years old." Blue eyes twinkling, she leaned down to Samuel and whispered, "That's even older than Grandma." She straightened and inhaled the green. "So old, yet so alive."

Dad put an arm around mom, pulled her to his side, and kissed her cheek. Then he took Samuel's hand and tugged him along the soft, needle-matted trail. "Come on, son."

Samuel wanted none of that. Craning his neck, walking backwards, he pointed and wailed, "Giants!"

"Lots more giants to see up here," dad insisted. "Let's keep moving."

Samuel walked backwards until they passed around the next bend, then turned and shuffled along with downcast eyes.

A rustle stirred the treetops behind as a great brown hand gently parted the branches above, as a huge green eye peered through the gap at the now-empty trail, as a great sigh stirred the leaves. Then the branches swished back into place. A Stellar's jay cried somewhere among the trees, and the deep silence of the forest closed in.

Falling Star

The first to hit the floor was a pale blue sphere laced with silver swirls and dusted with glitter. The plastic ornament bounced on the hardwood with a hollow knock and rolled until it came to rest against a chair leg, leaving a faint trail of sparkles. The tree shivered and jingled while the ornament undertook this pilgrimage. Mephisto, naturally, was long gone by the time the bauble came to rest.

"Stupid cat," Ruth muttered as she rehung the ornament.

The next to go was a string of lights, or the portion thereof draped across the lowest branches on the left, which became tangled with Mephisto's paw and refused to relinquish its grip until he'd dragged it a foot off the branch. The tree shook as though fending off an arctic blast, but somehow no ornament lost its grip.

"This," Ruth's husband Martin grumbled while restoring the lights to their rightful position, "is why we can't have a *nice* tree."

"It's nice," Ruth said, although not with conviction. "It's just . . ."

Martin stepped back to inspect the repairs. "Cheap. And weird."

She couldn't deny it. Every ornament from apex down was shatterproof plastic. The bottom two tiers of fake foliage stretched out bare except for the lights. No point in decorating them. Mephisto would have scattered all such low-hanging ornaments around the house in record time. And forget tinsel, which if ingested by the feline would play havoc with his intestines.

"Still." Ruth sidled up to Martin and slipped her arms around him.

"I guess," he grudgingly agreed.

The next day, Mephisto slithered up the wood dowel trunk to the fourth branch on the left which bent under his weight, displacing a green teardrop, a silver sphere, and a snowman Vicki had made nine years ago in second grade, not to mention gnarling a length of lights. The crime occurred in the middle of the day when only old Al, Ruth's father, was home. Reading or sleeping through one of his history books, he hadn't witnessed anything. Vicki arrived home from school, made a sandwich, and shuttered herself in her room with her cell phone and tablet computer. She had nothing to report, either. Ruth and Martin only discovered the crime scene after work. Martin spent ten minutes ungnarling, rearranging, and rehanging while Al slept in the recliner across the room, covered in a cheery red and green blanket, and Mephisto slept in Al's lap.

"Chicken wire," Martin suggested at dinner.

Ruth, ladling out chili, paused. Drops dripped back into the steaming pan. "What?"

"Chicken wire. For the tree." He made an encircling motion with his finger.

Ruth rolled her eyes and continued serving.

Vicki swiped her phone a few times. "We don't have chickens, Dad."

"I didn't say—"

Al peered into his bowl as his daughter filled it. "Bad idea, bringing chickens into a house with a cat." He inhaled deeply and smiled. "This looks good, Ruthy."

Martin shook his head. "Forget it. I'll think of something else."

Vicki made a face and changed the subject. "I have to do a science thing tonight. Can you help me, Dad?"

Ruth finished serving and sat down. Martin lifted a spoonful of chili and gently blew on it. The steam enveloped his face. "Calculating how many cats fit in a Christmas tree?"

Having perfected the "my Dad is the stupidest man in the world" look, Vicki gave it to him. "No. Meteors."

"How many meteors fit in a Christmas tree?"

"No! Counting meteors! In the sky! There's supposed to be a meteor shower tonight. See?" She shoved her phone at him.

Martin read the assignment. "Geminids. Radiant. Hourly rate. Best seen a couple hours before dawn! What, the teacher wants you kids to stay up all night?"

"You could call me in sick tomorrow," Vicki suggested.

"Dream on." He reread the assignment. "Dark skies? Where are we supposed to find *those*? So you get to spend an hour freezing to death searching a light-polluted sky for meteors you won't be able to see. Brilliant."

Vicki snatched her phone back. "Fine, don't help me."

"I didn't say that. We'll go out at eleven. We might get lucky."

Ruth looked up. "Eleven? When's she supposed to sleep?"

"*I* didn't give her the assignment."

Before Ruth could further object, a cacophony of clattering ornaments sounded in the living room.

Al blew on a spoonful of chili and chuckled. "I told you not to name that cat after the devil."

A light snowfall the day before left half an inch of powder coating the grass, dotted with a few footprints from passing critters. Clear, cold air followed. Bundled in their winter coats, hats, and gloves, Martin and Vicki dragged a pair of lawn chairs onto the driveway, sat, and looked up. Gradually their eyes adjusted to the not-quite dark of suburbia. Above, a handful of brilliant stars dotted the heavens, connected by lesser points of light.

"Your Grandpa taught me some of this," Martin said, pointing. "Let's see if I remember. There's Orion. That's Sirius, the Dog Star, and Aldeberan, the eye of Taurus. Those stars around Aldeberan are the Hyades, and up there, the Pleiades. Over there is Capella, and right there's what we're looking for. Gemini, the twins. Pollux is the brighter star, Castor the other. The meteors will appear to come from right about there. Not bad for an old man, huh?"

Vicki's fingers, shoved deep into her pockets, itched for her cell phone.

Father and daughter sat silent in the night, accompanied by nothing but stars and an occasional passing car. Fifteen minutes passed. Twenty minutes. Thirty. More. Nothing.

"I'm cold," Vicki said. "Let's go in."

Martin shivered. "Give it an hour at least."

"Why?"

"How can you report an hourly rate if you don't give it at least an hour?"

"By multiplying zero by two."

Why, Martin wondered, *are you only clever when trying to wiggle out of something?*

They watched the sky for another ten minutes. The stars only twinkled. Nothing fell.

"Dad, let's just—"

A blaze of light flashed overhead. Vicki gasped. Martin's breath caught in his throat. It lasted but two seconds, then was gone, but it felt portentous, a promise of great things to come.

They waited, but no. Just the one.

Gradually, they relaxed. The show was over. But what a show it had been.

"Zero times two equals one," Martin chided.

"Shut up, Dad."

He smiled in the dark.

The following evening, Mephisto resumed his career of destruction. His next incursion breached the fifth circle of branches, bent another two boughs, and sparked a rain of ornaments onto the floor. The cacophony brought Martin, Ruth, and Vicki on the run, and even woke up old Al, who as usual had been snoozing in the recliner, that cheery red and green blanket covering his lap. Mephisto tumbled to the floor and dematerialized while the tree tottered. Martin gathered it into his arms like a giant child just in time to prevent its felling. Fake needles poked his face and filled his mouth. Sputtering, he righted the tree, but not before the topper toppled. Helpless, they all watched the star plummet and bounce across the floor.

"This time," Martin decreed, "he's gone too far!" Steadying the tree, he inspected the misaligned and broken branches. "That's the Star of Bethlehem he's defiled!"

Ruth bent down to gather up the scattered ornaments. She waved Vicki over to help, since Martin was basically useless when angry. "It's just a piece of plastic, dear. No harm done."

"You call this no harm?" Martin's hands flailed erratically at the tree. Vicki sniggered. "What's so funny, young lady? What's at *all* funny?"

"Falling star," she said. "Just like last night." She covered her mouth and chuckled some more, then picked up the ornament and handed it to her father.

Martin huffed and inspected it for damage. "The Star of Bethlehem was *not* a falling star."

Al leaned forward in his chair. "Certainly not. A falling star is like us, just a flash in the pan."

Although the old man retained most of his marbles, he had his moments, so Martin ignored him. He presented the star for all to see. "How about that. It actually is shatterproof. I guess this won't be its last year, after all."

"Well, of course not." Al tugged the blanket around his shoulders. Mephisto instantly rematerialized and jumped into his lap. He scratched the cat behind the ears. "Even you can't destroy it. Can you?"

The Crossing

He'd put this off until the last minute not because he was in mourning but so he didn't seem greedy. There was enough talk in the town and among Sarah's relatives already. But she was dead, nothing could bring her back, and she had left everything to him. Now papers must be filed, which meant a long ride to his lawyer's office in Ganttsville, the county seat.

So Walter was up before dawn, got himself about, and saddled up his white mare Primrose. He settled his Stetson on his head, stuffed the sheaf of papers—his future—into the saddlebag and led the horse into the orange morning glow. Sunlight glinted from the distant snow-capped range while the wind breathed warm through the grasses and trees of the valley. Sarah's valley. His valley now, in all but law, and soon that would be fixed. His home, his ranch, his livelihood.

All his.

He nudged Primrose forward. Dew sparkled in the meadow. Breeze and birdsong accompanied him down the road, calling up memories of another day, a day of sun and warmth much like this, a day of joy and laughter and song but two years before when he and Sarah married. Sarah was her father's only child, but her extended family flocked to the wedding. They had money and he didn't, but he was working on it. He had learned the banking trade from the ground up, and his prospects for advancement were strong. Thankfully, it made no difference to Sara or her father that Walter hadn't yet made his fortune. She was madly in love, and her father respected Walter's business acumen.

She married Walter for love, but he married her for money. Yes, he was fond of Sarah, but she hadn't been his only prospect. Tall, strong, and young, he could have had any woman in the territory. Before meeting her, his eye had been on a considerable few beauties and his hands on several. None, though, had Sarah's prospective wealth. He could make do with lesser passion to gain greater means. Her father's wealth already flowed to her, and in time she would inherit everything. Then it would be as good as Walter's. That day simply came sooner than expected. Sarah's father fell victim to a hunting accident within a year of their marriage, and not six months later, she miscarried and died.

The sun crept higher while Primrose clopped along the dirt track and Walter reflected on these events. Was he was wicked, no longer feeling the loss, indeed feeling liberated by becoming the master of all Sarah had owned? No. Surely it was right to be glad. He paid dearly, burying wife and child, mourning their loss. Now was the time to dry the tears and make a new life. He couldn't undo what was done, and in truth he had been given a gift. He was still young, his prospects never better. He could enjoy new women, might even marry again. Who could say? Some of the women he had once eyed and held were still about and unwed. Others had married, but not all happily. He might ease their sufferings from time to time. Yes, things had turned out well, after all.

Lost in such fancies, Walter came to the river that snaked through the valley, its broad, shallow course hidden from view by tall grasses and a scattering of trees. He heard the water before he saw it. It bubbled softly, barely louder than the wind, clean and comforting. He reigned in his horse and listened. The wind picked up the rhythm of the water, and within moments the sounds merged into a song, quiet, insistent, a pleasant background to his dreams of the future. Then he heard words faint against the breeze, words to a familiar song, dark and forlorn. Walter pushed up the brim of his hat and listened. Why would such a cheerful river sing those words?

> *From father to mother, from sister to brother,*
> *From cousin to cousin, they're cheating each other.*
> *Since cheating has grown to be so much the fashion,*
> *I believe to my soul it will run the whole Nation,*
> *And it's hard, hard times.*

Foreboding tingled in Walter's spine. The singing wasn't wind and water after all. It was a woman with a voice as thin as the breeze and distant as the mountains. Drawing a breath, he spurred his horse on and passed through the grasses to the muddy bank.

The river took a sharp bend. The woman sat in the water, dead center, clothed in sodden white, glowing as though a fragment of the sun reposed within the folds of her bodice. Her golden hair, too, shown with sunlight, and her skin was as white as yarrow blossoms. She gazed into the water rippling by her waist as though tracking a fish swimming about her thighs, oblivious to Walter's presence. Her song continued, soft and low:

> *Now there is the talker, by talking he eats,*
> *And so does the butcher by killing his meats.*
> *He'll toss the steelyards, and weigh it right down,*
> *And swear it's just right if it lacks forty pounds, —*
> *And it's hard, hard times.*

His dread evaporated in the glow of her beauty. Transfixed, Walter spurred Primrose forward into the water. The horse stopped after but three steps. A voice deep in his mind told him to keep going, to cross the river and ride on, to get those papers delivered, but he couldn't take his eyes from the woman, couldn't speak even to say hello. He wanted her but couldn't reach out a hand to touch her.

She lifted her eyes, and they were as blue as the sky. Neither startled by his presence nor embarrassed by the lust etched on his face, she continued to sing:

> *And there is the merchant, as honest, we're told.*
> *Whatever he sells you, my friend, you are sold;*
> *Believe what I tell you, and don't be surprised*
> *To find yourself cheated half out of your eyes,*
> *And it's hard, hard times.*

Her voice stilled. Walter, feeling a fool, cleared his throat but found nothing to say.

"Where do you go, sir?" she asked.

He swallowed.

The water swirled about her hips. She rose and stood in the middle of the river, dripping, pale, her translucent dress clinging to her body, revealing every exquisite curve and exposing the darkness of her nipples. "Where do you go, sir?" she repeated.

Primrose shied away. Walter nudged her forward again and found his voice at last. "I might sit here forever, ma'am, looking at you." *Or take you to my bed and have everything a man could want.* The unspoken thought woke the voice that had prompted him to ride on: *Fool! You have nothing until your errand is complete!* "But I'm heading into town today," he added, his voice rimed with sadness. "I return tomorrow. Could I see you then?"

"You see me now, sir."

I do, as well as if you were naked.

She might have heard the thought. She smiled, coy, and held out a beckoning hand.

Drawn by her summons, Walter dismounted. He knew he shouldn't. He should get on with his business and find her when he returned. Yet warnings echoed in his ears. *Don't trust her! Where is her horse? Where did she come from? Why is she here?*

He didn't listen. He couldn't. He was in the water before he realized it, sloshing toward her. Their fingertips touched. She took his hand and drew him near.

He touched her fingers, her arms, her face, her shoulders, her hips. "How long have you been in the river?" he asked. "You're freezing!"

"Then warm me, sir."

She slipped her arms about his waist and pressed her body to his. His hands roamed her while cold damp seeped into his clothing. He touched his lips to her frigid mouth. She pushed away but held him still and slid down to the water like a rag doll. He tried to hold her up, to keep her from the water, but she grew heavy and they both sank to their knees. She laid back in the water, sank under the water and drew him down, locked in a tight embrace. Then they were splashing, rolling together, sinking and rising, laughing at their folly. Her fingers tickled his sides. He laughed and she laughed, and she tickled him again and again, nonstop, laughing, pulling him under, pushing him up, pulling down again, laughing above the water, breathing in the water and laughing and tickling and laughing while he struggled against her, breath held, eyes wild, pushing away but unable to escape her grasping laughing tickling suffocating embrace.

On the riverbank, Primrose screamed. A great upwelling of water erupted, and she ran, terrified, for home.

The water stilled. The woman surfaced. She ran her fingers through her hair to untangle it and gazed into the water as though tracking a fish swimming about her thighs.

A song whispered through the valley.

> *And there's the young widow, coquettish and shy,*
> *With a smile on her lips and a tear in her eye,*
> *But when she gets married she'll cut quite a dash,*
> *She'll give him the reins and she'll handle the cash,*
> *And it's hard, hard times.*

Walter's hat floated by. The woman lifted it from the water, shook it, and cast it away.

Zoë

Evening fell hard that night. Its blackness descended while, oblivious, I fought to balance my overdrawn checking account. Outside, the night-chatter of frogs and hum of insects rose in the dark. I neither heard nor felt their presence until, an hour after sunset with an orange gibbous moon rising in the east, I pushed back from my computer, ran my hand through my scraggly, sandy hair, and gave up. Only then did I noticed them, their calls enveloping me like the chatter of old friends. Increasingly these nights, I felt grateful for their unseen companionship. Aside from them, I had no one. I had moved out here three years ago to the middle of nowhere, Montana to get away from people, but sometimes, when the night closed in, I longed for someone to talk to.

At first, life here had seemed idyllic. Back in Denver, I'd known nothing but loss and irritation. No family left, no true friends, not even any colleagues I particularly liked. A failed law student, for twelve years I'd shuffled papers and appointment calendars for a modest law firm. It paid well enough, but the grind and office politics wore me down. I ended each day feeling like I'd been run over by a sixteen-wheeler. I tried to lie to myself, tried to convince myself it would get better, that personnel changes would moderate the politics, that the workload would ease. But no. Finally I realized the insanity of contenting myself with discontent. I chucked it all—job, condo, everything—and fled here to make a living off the internet.

No, I didn't go off half-cocked. I planned my upheaval. I hatched a scheme to earn money writing legal blog posts, supplemented by advertising. I even wrote up a business plan. I just hadn't realized how hard it was to translate dreams into reality. And now? After three years of struggle, insolvency loomed as large as the rising moon. What I needed, I thought with some desperation, was a guardian angel to knock on my door and fix all my problems.

Yes, I actually thought that, leaning on my elbows at the kitchen table, staring into my laptop screen, hiding in my cabin in the woods. I nearly fell out of my chair when immediately someone hammered on the door and a woman's voice, brimming with desperation, cried, "Is anybody home?"

The coincidence was too much. I felt my insides flip but could only stare at the door. The pounding subsided for a moment before resuming with increased vigor. "Please, is anyone there?"

Her plea moved me to action. I hurried to the door and flipped on the porch light. Without removing the chain, I cracked the door. I'm not sure what I expected to see. A tall, ethereal beauty affixed with white billowing wings, maybe.

In fact she was rather small, only five foot five including the thick brown hair flowing over the crown of her head and pulled back in a ponytail. Her dark eyes blinked at me in astonishment, or maybe fear. Dressed in a short green skirt and white blouse, she clutched a little white purse before her with both hands.

"I'm sorry," she nearly cried. "I'm really sorry."

Feeling like an idiot scared of his own reflection, I undid the chain and eased the door open. "For what?"

"Do you have a land line? I can't get any reception out here."

I peered into the night but couldn't see a vehicle. She must have had car trouble out on the road, I supposed. My cabin was set a quarter mile up a gravel drive. Nobody would walk up here in the dark by choice.

Whoever she was, she didn't seem dangerous, so I opened the door wide. "Yeah, come on in." While she scanned my spartan one-room as though it hid mortal traps, I closed the door behind her and refastened the chain. "Car trouble?"

"Ran out of gas. Stupid of me, but I really thought there would be a gas station."

I gave the room a once-over, too, fearing it might be too messy for such a pretty visitor. The kitchen in the back corner wasn't exactly choked with dirty dishes, but I hadn't cleaned it up today. My bed in the opposite corner—a queen because I tended to flop around in my sleep—was unmade but didn't look too disreputable. Although I hadn't yet lit a fire in the tiny stone fireplace, uncleaned soot and ash had accumulated there. Its smell suffused the air.

Her nose wrinkled as though she had only just noticed. "You live here alone?"

Wasn't it obvious? "Yeah. Here's the phone." I led her to the kitchen and retrieved the device from the table.

She took it and studied it as though she'd never seen one before. "I just realized, I don't know who to call."

"Family?" I suggested. "A friend?"

She shrugged. "Don't have any."

"Me, either." As soon as I said it, I wished I hadn't. I had no interest in forming bonds, however tenuous. "I don't suppose you're a triple-A member?"

She shook her head. "I'm pretty hopeless, I guess. Do you have any gas, like for a lawn mower?"

"Afraid not." I didn't bother telling her lawn mowers were of little use in a forest.

She pulled out a chair. Although distraught, she slipped into the seat as easily as if it were her own kitchen. "I guess I'm stuck."

"Don't worry. I'll find emergency service for you online." I sat around the corner from her, in front of my laptop. Only then did I realize uncleared dishes from dinner—and lunch, and breakfast—cluttered the table. I pushed as much of it aside as I could to give her room. "Sorry about the mess."

She regarded the clutter without much interest. "I guess it doesn't seem so important when it's just you."

"Depends on the day." I entered search terms into the computer and located the one and only roadside emergency service in our area, a place over thirty miles away. "Here we go. It'll take them a little while to get here." I turned the computer so she could see the number.

"Thanks." She turned away as if by so doing she might secure her privacy. I heard the beep of numbers being punched into the phone, then she set the device to her ear. "Hi, I ran out of gas. Could you send someone out?" She listened, gave our location, listened some more, and signed off with a resigned, "Okay, thanks."

She handed the phone back and gazed at the darkness beyond the kitchen window. "Three hours." She sounded miserable.

I couldn't send her out into that dark to wait on her own, yet I didn't want company. I came out here to get away from people. *Why*, I asked nobody, *did this woman have to run out of gas here of all places?*

She glanced at me as though she'd heard. It was stupid, but the fear that she might be able to peer into my mind embarrassed me. "You can stay here," I offered by way of contrition. "I'll walk you to your car when the time comes."

She smiled gratefully while objecting, "You don't have to do that."

"It's okay." Which it wasn't, not exactly. Yet my shame at having wished her away melted in her smile, and I realized how good it felt to have someone understand. Assuming she did. I might have been imagining it. But so what? If nothing else, sheltering her would give me an excuse to ignore my financial mess until tomorrow. "You want something? Coffee? Tea?"

"Coffee would be nice." Her smile persisted, warmed me, and I found myself returning it. "But really, I don't want to be a bother."

"It's no bother." I got up, flipped on the coffee maker, and took a pair of mugs from a cupboard.

"Sure it is. You don't like people, do you? I'm an unwanted intrusion."

I felt myself flush. She could read my mind, after all! "I'm a bit of a loner, I guess."

"Where are your parents?"

"Dead. Their house burned down. Faulty wiring, the fire inspector said." As the coffee dripped through the machine, I turned to face her. I'd answered automatically and wished I hadn't. I didn't want to open that wound, not tonight, not in front of a complete stranger. In fact, we'd missed a few steps in the process. Why hadn't we introduced ourselves? "What's your name?"

She gave me a coy smile. "What's yours?"

"I asked first."

"So you did. No brothers or sisters, I guess?"

I shook my head and turned away. The interrogation should have irritated me, but I couldn't manage anger. Her questions forced me to acknowledge the deep hollow in the pit of my stomach, a void carved out of me years before.

"No woman in your life?"

"Thankfully not."

She laughed. "Can't live with 'em, can't live without 'em?"

Why would she ask that? Did she have designs on me already? Had I sparked her pity, ignited her interest, or inadvertently fanned her desire? I couldn't see how, but such thoughts imposed themselves upon me anyway while the coffee finished brewing. Forcing a few breaths to steady myself, I poured and brought the steaming mugs to the table. "They can't seem to live with me. Best you don't even think about it."

"Hmm." She took the mug in both hands. Her face melted in ecstasy at its warmth. "I'm not thinking anything. You're the one who called me."

Not understanding, I watched her drink the whole mug in one long swallow, steam curling about her face, her eyes never leaving mine. She had beautiful eyes, eyes you could fall into and never find your way out of. "What's your name?" I asked again.

"Take your pick. I have so many. "

She held out her mug to ask for more coffee. I hadn't touched mine yet and found I had no interest in it, so I pushed it to her. "Your real one will do."

     In the Realm of Tiny Giants

With a nod of thanks, she wrapped her hands around the mug and lifted it to her lips. She blew on the steam. "Zoë."

I laughed, probably because I'd been expecting something more common, like Susan or Mary. "Like the second Doctor Who's companion? You don't look a thing like her."

"*She* was named after *me*." Zoë drank down her second mug in one protracted gulp, then delicately wiped her mouth with the back of her hand. "Who do I look like?"

I didn't know, but something about the shape of her face and the turn of her mouth reminded me a bit of my mother. A fragment of anguish rose in my throat and tried to choke me. I forced it back down. "I have a strange feeling you know. In fact, I'll bet you know a lot more about me than I know about you. How is that possible?"

She held out the mug. "I don't want to impose, but . . ."

I got up and gave her a refill, which she downed as quickly as the first two. Then, setting the mug gently on the table, she rose. "I should go. If I stay, I'll run you out of coffee."

"Go where? You need gas."

"Nah, I just said that so you'd open the door."

She crossed the room and started to undo the chain on the front door, her movements slow, elegant, hypnotizing. I suddenly realized I didn't want her to go. I didn't know why. I only knew that if she left the night would close in again, and I couldn't take that anymore. So I rushed after her. "Wait! I don't know who you are. I don't even know *what* you are!" Reaching her, I put my hand on hers to keep her from turning the knob.

"Oh, so now you want me to stay."

Her rebuke jarred me as though she'd slapped my face. "I . . ."

She smiled and enfolded my hand in hers. "For now, that's enough."

A moment later I was alone, not remembering when or how she had slipped through the door, or even if she had. She could have dissolved into mist and floated up the chimney for all I knew. And yet, even though she was gone, somehow she lingered. Here at the door. There at the kitchen table. In the smell of the coffee and the chirp of frogs in the night. She filled the place, and so I knew she wouldn't be on the road when the emergency service drove by. I checked my phone's call list, thinking I should tell them not to bother, but I couldn't pull up the number. No call had been placed that night

Still, Zoë was *real*. She lingered for days, never out of my thoughts. I wondered who she was, where she lived, how I might find her. I looked for her online, but with only a first name it was a fool's quest. Could she live in a nearby town? I forced myself to venture out of the cabin to find her, but to no avail. I talked with servers in mom and pop restaurants, with gas station attendants, with librarians, with the well-to-do and the poor going about their daily business. Nobody had ever heard of Zoë or anyone quite fitting her description. Not with her thirst for coffee, anyway.

Now, a strange thing happened while I searched. As people learned who I was, I started to help some of them. While not a lawyer, I knew something of the law, and from time to time someone would ask advice. I could at least guide them to services or answer basic questions.

The further I ventured, the more I gave, the less I craved solitude. Not that I abandoned my cabin. It remained a safe retreat at the end of the day, surrounded by the sounds of night creatures, the crackle of a fire, the smell of coffee, and the memory of Zoë's smile. Yet I began to see I needed others at least a little, and just possibly others needed me in turn.

Because of Zoë, I'm rediscovering the world. But then, how could it be otherwise? For I know what she is now. She's not just any woman. She's . . .

Oh, you'd never believe me. Go look her up for yourself.

The Gift of Empathy

I

I found him when he didn't want to be found, so of course it didn't end well.

I'm a reporter. Call me by my pen name, Jess Williams. I've used it for so long I sometimes wonder how I remember my real name anymore. I scrounge up human interest stories for the only surviving newspaper in a city of modest size, and what could be of more interest to humans than somebody who understands their pain? Most of us spend half our waking lives hoping to meet such a someone, and there he was, just down the street and around the corner.

At least, that's what Alice Corman told me when I took her story. Alice had lost three husbands in seven years, putting the lie to the superstition about the luck of seven. She had three children, ages eleven, eight, and four, one by each of her deceased men, and had run afoul of the state's demented family services regulations. If she ventured into the world of work to support her kids, they'd be taken from her for neglect. If she stayed home, cared for them, and collected government money, she could raise them in comfortable poverty and earn the scorn of those who branded her a freeloader. And yet, when I asked her to describe her life, she stunned me with a single word.

"Blessed." She said it like a whisper of cool wind on a warm summer day.

"You look skeptical," she laughed, and I had to confess I was. Here we sat on her battered, third-hand sofa surrounded by a meager collection of other people's castoffs, she clothed in Goodwill Store chic and me in my pantsuit and heels. She hardly looked blessed, not from what I could see. Easier to assume she was lying to get my attention.

"I know," she admitted. "I wouldn't have used that word myself three years ago. But then I met Harvey Jennings."

She'd said it like she expected me to know the man, but of course I didn't. "Who's Harvey Jennings?" I took a sip of the weak iced tea she had offered me.

"A gifted man. Maybe the most remarkable man in the world."

Superlatives, I silently scolded, *will get you nowhere*. "Gifted how?"

Her smile suggested enigma, but whether the puzzle was her or Harvey, who could say? Alice wasn't yet ready for the reveal. "You wouldn't understand. I'll have to tell you the story."

Stories are my life. I could splash the most tragic tale across the page and collect my fee without remorse. But here I suspected I'd been suckered into recording fantasy. Alice Corman, broken woman, desperate, slipping over the edge of madness. How she must crave company, long for a sympathetic ear, and I had been elected, sympathetic or not.

We make so many bad assumptions, don't we?

Alice huffed as she lifted the basket overflowing with sodden laundry and waddled to the bank of dryers. She dropped it there. When it smacked the floor, she stared as though scolding it for making such racket, but her plain, round face couldn't quite manage the proper disgust. Her dark skin glowed just enough in the harsh light of the laundromat to soften the bite of her pinched lips and narrowed eyes. However bad or mad she felt inside, she could never manage to look more than ill.

Opening the dryer, she shoveled the kids' clothes in. She could hear her children playing on the opposite side of the facility, Theresa reading loudly from a Dr. Seuss book in a brave effort to divert the attention of Andrew and especially Mary, the youngest, from the temptations of rows and rows of machines with flashing lights and pressable buttons.

Once the dryer had been fed its money and undertook its chore, she turned and watched the kids. This wasn't what she'd had planned, neither for them nor herself. Before life beat her up and left her bleeding on the floor, she'd had plans. A future. Now she could see no further than the number of days her monthly handout would last. How could she give the kids any hope at all? God, was she exhausted.

The laundromat wasn't busy at this hour. A handful of other mothers, some with children in tow, worked mostly in silence. Only one man was present, an older fellow sitting by the window, dressed in navy slacks and a pale blue button-down shirt, absorbed in a paperback. His ashen face reminded Alice of the presidents carved on Mt. Rushmore, but as she watched, his mouth twitched from time to time and he occasionally squeezed his eyes shut.

And once or twice, he stole a glance at Theresa.

Biting her lip, Alice hurried to her children and sat next to Theresa, who continued reading without glancing up. Alice kept her eyes on the man and caught him twice more stealing a look before deciding she'd had enough. She went directly to him, drew herself up although she was barely five seven, and made her best effort at a motherly glare.

The man pulled the book closer to his face and said nothing.

"I see you looking at my daughter," Alice snapped, louder than necessary.

A few other mothers shot them a surprised look, but the man continued reading, or pretended to. From the cover, Alice thought it must be a science book. She didn't know what else to say, but given how he purposely ignored her, the message had been received. She turned to go back.

"She's growing up fast," the man said, a tremor in his aging voice, his eyes still buried in his book.

How dare you! Alice spun and raised her hand to strike. Not that she could ever hit anyone, but maybe the threat would warn him off.

"I only mean Theresa is very responsible."

Alice froze, hand still raised. "How do you know her name?"

The man shrugged. "I know things."

"That's no answer."

"I don't like it, either, Alice. Sometimes I hate it. Yesterday evening, I hauled my burden up to the roof of my apartment building and nearly pitched it over the edge."

Her hand dropped. She squinted at him, a vague sense of recognition niggling at her. "What's your name?"

"Harvey." He paused just enough to prompt her, but before she could ask, he added, "Jennings."

"Who's Harvey Jennings?"

"Right now, he's an old man waiting for his laundry to dry." Harvey's eyes didn't rise from his book, not once, not even to acknowledge her presence, but he settled the volume in his lap, apparently no longer needing to hide in it.

"Look at me," Alice demanded.

He shook his head.

"Look at me, and don't you lie. I'll know if you're lying. What do you want with my Theresa?"

Still Harvey refused to lift his eyes, but he laughed bitterly. "*You* would know? If only!" He raised the book again, then lowered it with a sigh. "I want nothing with Theresa or you or anyone else. I wish you'd all go away."

Alice set her hands to her hips, hoping she'd look severe that way. "That's why you keep looking at her, huh?"

"No." He chewed his lip, eyes still on the book in his lap, then shook his head as though exhausted. "Fine. Sit."

Although Alice didn't want to sit next to this man, curiosity got the better of her. She warily sat one chair over from him and waited.

Harvey rubbed his forehead and mouthed words he didn't speak, like a speaker trying to memorize his lines. "I feel things," he finally said.

"Things? Like what?"

"Everything. Your loss. Your sorrow. Your anger." He waved a hand about to indicate the whole laundromat. "Everyone's." He licked his lips and shook his head again. "Especially yours. Especially your fear. It devours your insides. You hide it, fight it, and some days you win, but most days you call it no better than a draw."

Alice sat petrified.

"Tell me I'm wrong."

She couldn't, for he wasn't.

"Of course, I'm not. I never am." Harvey slapped his book. "Never!"

Shivering like a cornered mouse, Alice whispered, "Is that why you almost killed yourself?"

He leaned back and closed his eyes. "Imagine," he began, but no further words came.

Alice, though, had patience if nothing else, and waited him out.

Eventually, he tried again. "Imagine you're watching a house on fire, and every time the fames lick the curtains, devour a table, feast on a wall, something inside of you incinerates, too."

Alice covered her mouth and turned away. Such horrid, horrid lies! Why would he say such a thing?

"You want to put out your fire, Alice?" Harvey opened his book and flipped pages without reading. "Stop pining for what's lost. Your future is *there*." Harvey nodded toward Theresa, who had managed to corral her younger siblings and moved on to the next book. The three of them turned pages together, pointing, making silly comments about silly drawings, and laughing.

Alice smiled at them until his words caught up with her. "How dare you judge me! What do *you* know about my life?"

"What I said. Every last detail, every last sensation, every last thought, every last emotion." He closed his eyes and tapped his chest. "It's all in here. Don't ask how. I don't know. It just is. I wish it wasn't." When he opened his eyes again, tears glistened in the corners, but whether for her or himself she didn't know. He drew a ragged breath and pulled the book to his face again. "Now go away. Leave me alone."

Alice stared at him while he buried himself in the pages. Then she rejoined her children and listened to Theresa read while Andrew and Mary tossed out more silly comments. Sometime later, when she went to check on her laundry, Harvey Jennings was gone.

II

I didn't believe Alice Corman's story. Of course not. But I wrote it up anyway, and after some heated words with my editor Kaycee — Katrina Celeste Petrosky, but we all called her Kaycee—she agreed it would run with only minor changes. Unfortunately, Kaycee's blessing only came with a curse.

"One date, Jess. Dinner, maybe a movie, just to get him out of his funk. I promise he won't bother you after that." She arched her eyebrows, indicating this was no request. It was fair payment for acquiescing to my demands.

Her assurances notwithstanding, in my experience men didn't give up that easily. Plus I knew her younger brother Karl, sort of. I'd met him at the newspaper's Family Day festivities the previous summer. He had a well-endowed brunette named Martina hanging on his arm that day while his eyes roamed freely over the field and settled more than once on me. His lady friend either didn't notice or didn't care that he had interests beyond her. Karl himself was the sort to attract attention: a fit six foot two with dark, wavy hair and a brilliant, perpetual smile on his lips. When Kaycee introduced us, I admit I felt a quiver inside, and afterward I couldn't remember a thing we had said to each other.

But quivers notwithstanding, I wasn't about to become Karl's next conquest. I'd let myself be conquered and pillaged and burned to the ground twice before, which was more than enough for one lifetime. So to hell with him.

"Martina dumped him," Kaycee explained. "No warning at all. He came home one day and her stuff was gone. She left a note that said nothing, no reason, just that it was over and he shouldn't try to find her."

"When was this?"

"Three months ago. He's been moping around ever since, like his whole life is over. Just be nice to him, okay?"

Like I have a choice, I grumbled. But maybe I could get a story out of it.

By strange coincidence, Karl and I met for dinner the day my story about Alice Corman and Harvey Jennings ran. I didn't bother reading it. When I was a cub reporter, I eagerly awaited the sight of my name and words in print, but now I didn't need validation. I got my story, wrote it up, turned it in, and moved on to the next thing. I might not even have remembered had it not been for Karl.

Dressed in charcoal slacks and a blue striped shirt open at the collar, he looked as dashing as I remembered, except his smile had run off to places unknown. To be fair, he pretended fairly well. He arrived at my condo at five-thirty, presented me with a single yellow rose, and said it was good to see me again. Not wanting to signal the wrong thing, or much of anything, really, I wore a conservative green knee-length dress and had pulled my light brown hair back in a ponytail. The yellow rose of friendship aside, we looked like a couple of middle managers *en route* to a pointless business meeting.

He took me to a family-owned Italian joint I knew by reputation only. It was supposed to be good and a bit pricey. Once we were seated with drinks in hand and food ordered—lasagna for him, seafood primavera for me—he gave me a searching look. "I liked your story today."

"Thank you. It was a strange one, wasn't it?"

"I guess." He unfolded his napkin and toyed with the edges, studying them as though the secret to life might be sewn into the hem.

"What did you like about it?" Not that I cared, but I had to say something, even though it felt like interviewing him rather than talking to him.

He shrugged while he mulled it over. "The happy ending, I guess."

I don't know what it was. Maybe the misery dripping from his voice. Maybe the vacant look in his eyes. Or maybe even though I knew better, some part of me longed to feel again that sensation he'd ignited in me last year. Whatever it was, when I opened my mouth, what came out was at best atypical, at worst syrupy. "I think we make our own happy endings. We could try to be happy this evening, anyway." I'm usually nowhere near that supportive.

Karl looked up, his lips pinched. "Oh yeah? When you don't want to be here with me?"

That hit too close to the mark for comfort. "Why do you say that?"

"Because of last summer."

I hoped I hadn't said something stupid at the time, but I really had no idea.

"Women are such paradoxes. You're afraid of the very men who excite you. I did excite you, at least a little, didn't I? So now you don't want to be anywhere near me. Don't bother denying it."

I didn't, but only because I had no idea what he was talking about, or at least that's what I told myself. Unfortunately, my silence only confirmed whatever impression he'd formed of me. He stopped fidgeting with his napkin, leaned forward, and gave me a dull look. "It's all right. I'm not in the market anyway. I want something else from you."

I patted my mouth with my napkin while I tried to find my lost composure. "Like what?"

"To meet Harvey Jennings. Can you arrange that?"

My stress bubble burst so suddenly I couldn't help laughing, loud and nearly hysterical. People looked. Some grinned, some scowled. The waitress arrived with our meals, cracked a smile, caught the infection, and laughed along with me. Sliding the hot plates in front of us, she said, "Sorry I missed *that* joke."

Once she was out of the way, Karl frowned at his lasagna. "I'm serious."

"Come on, Karl. Harvey Jennings is a figment of Alice Corman's imagination."

"Maybe, maybe not."

"He is. But even if he does exist, what could you possibly want with *him*?"

Karl stabbed at his meal but didn't take a bite.

He didn't need to explain. "You think he can fix you, impart some deep wisdom, cure your misery?"

He shrugged.

"That's just great. *I* can't make you happy, but a fantasy can." Which was a stupid thing to say. I hadn't agreed to this to make him happy, only to pay a debt to his sister. But I was steamed that he couldn't even pretend I might be pleasant company, so I didn't much care. Let him think what he would.

Which he did. "I could die in this chair and you wouldn't give a damn."

Now it was my turn to shut up and stare at my plate.

He reached across the table, palm upturned, begging to take my hand and apologize. "I'm sorry. That was stupid."

I didn't move or even look at him. To be honest, I wasn't sure what I was feeling at that moment. I could have slugged him or jumped into bed with him or just walked away. Or all three in rapid succession.

His hand remained outstretched. "Really, I'm sorry. Maybe you do care. If so, would you at least help me find out if this guy is real?"

It's hard not to pity a lost puppy. I gave him my hand and, although I knew better, nodded assent.

The rest of our play date passed in a silent fog. In fact, I took all but a few bites of my meal home in a box.

III

Two days later, I was hip deep in the hunt for Harvey Jennings. I'd searched news archives, public records, and social media without finding him. A lot of false leads surfaced, since the name isn't entirely uncommon. Wandering down blind alleys to dead ends, I'd made no progress.

Well, almost no progress. I did find a match on a driver's license that could have been him. Or not. According to the license, a Harvey Jennings lived in an isolated five-floor apartment building beyond the edge of the suburbs. Alice Corman's Harvey allegedly said he'd thought about jumping from the roof of his apartment building. Did that count as a connection? Or was it vapor?

While I was pondering the question that afternoon, Kaycee stopped by my desk to offer an update on her brother's condition. "I saw Karl yesterday evening. He's sounding a lot more positive. I told you you'd be good for him."

"Oh yeah," I agreed. "We're even getting married next week." I tried to keep excess sarcasm from my voice and make it sound like a joke but failed miserably.

She pushed back a stack of papers and sat on the edge of my desk, one of her more annoying habits. "Come on, it can't have been that bad, not from his perspective, anyway."

"So what did he tell you?"

"Nothing, just that it went fine."

"Fine, sure. Other than him giving me an irritating assignment. Maybe he's got your editor genes."

Kaycee didn't seem to know whether to laugh or snap back. She did a bit of both. "Let me guess. You're mad because he asked you to sleep with him. Or maybe because he didn't."

I wasn't about to take that bait, so my only option was to swipe at her via Karl. "He wants to talk to Harvey Jennings, so now I have to find him."

That shut her up. For a few moments, anyway. "The mythological guy from your story?"

"The same. If he's real, he's a ghost. There's almost no trace of him."

"So he's not real."

"Except maybe he lives here." I turned my computer monitor to show her a map overlaid with satellite imagery. I tapped the little red balloon marking the apartment building. "Some Harvey Jennings or another does. Could be him."

"Why would Karl want—" She leaned over and peered at the

map as though the answer might be found there.

"Come on, Kaycee, you know why. You read my article."

She thought about that. From the face she made, I figured she didn't like the obvious answer. Served her right. "Are you going?"

"I don't have much choice. If I don't, he'll get all blue again, and then you'll arrange another date for us."

Kaycee slid off the desk and gave me a lopsided smile. "I should anyway. Sounds like you could use one, or maybe two or three." She slunk away before I could reply.

Get far enough out, and suburbs fade into farmland. The concrete monstrosity matching the address I'd found might not have looked out of place here were it a silo rather than some developer's dream gone awry, but it wasn't. Five stories tall, grayish with just a splash of blue around the main entrance, fronted by a largely deserted parking lot, it seemed to beg for demolition.

I'd considered inviting Karl along. He deserved whatever disappointment was waiting here, the less than kind half of me suggested. But there wasn't much point until I knew whether this Harvey Jennings was our target. Likely he wasn't. So here I was, alone, walking into the cheerless lobby, checking the mailboxes for names, and finding almost nothing. If people lived here, they didn't advertise the fact. Not even Mr. Jennings.

I knew his number, though: 307. The building offered two means of ascent, a fairly creepy stairwell with insufficient lighting, an excess of litter, and smells you just don't want lingering where you're walking, or two elevators, one of which had an "Out of Order" sign hanging from it by a piece of yellowed tape. I decided it might be best not to test the functionality of the other, so I mounted the stairs, hoping no muggers lurked there. Arriving at my destination, I sucked in a deep breath and knocked.

No answer. I knocked again, and again, and again. I tried calling: "Mr. Jennings? Are you home?" But apparently not. Resigned to defeat,

I turned away, and only then saw the figure standing near the stairwell, old, pale, almost a statue, a book in one hand and a plastic grocery bag in the other.

"Mr. Jennings?" I asked, and he neither answered nor moved. Slowly, hands spread to indicate I meant no harm, I began to approach. "I'm Jess Williams. I'm a reporter. I wrote a story about—"

"I know who you are," he snapped. "Stay away from me."

"I just wanted to ask a favor, Mr. Jennings. For a friend."

He closed his eyes and wobbled as though he might pass out. "Back up. Let me get to my apartment."

I didn't understand. The hall wasn't terribly wide, but there was plenty of room.

"Back up," he repeated, so I did, and he slowly advanced until he reached his door. "Farther. Don't stand too near." Following instructions, I never got closer than fifteen feet, although I couldn't imagine why he feared me. He set his bag on the floor, fumbled for his keys, and slipped one into the lock.

I probably should have given up. Obviously Harvey Jennings had no intention of talking with me, and Karl was hardly my responsibility. Yet something strange happened as I watched this man. I felt something inside, like all the dark hollows in my soul filling with light, like whatever forces warred within me had declared a momentary truce. In that moment, I knew Alice Corman had told the truth. I knew that what Karl sought stood before me. And I knew I had to get through to Harvey Jennings.

"Please," I practically begged. "My friend needs your help."

"Don't give me that, Jess," Harvey snapped. He shoved the door open and picked up his bag. "And don't lie to yourself. Karl doesn't need *me.*" He hurried inside and slammed the door.

"But—" I called, hurrying to the door. The light fled. The war rekindled. I felt lost and helpless and alone. And angry. I pounded on the door. "You can't do this to me!"

"Are you *trying* to kill me?" Harvey cried, his voice stretched.

"Go away!"

I wouldn't. I couldn't. I pounded on the door again. "I just want to talk!"

Something slammed against the door. His fist, something he threw, I didn't know. "You wrote the damned article. Didn't you listen? Don't you know what you're doing to me?"

His words struck me with physical force. I backed away, seized with horror, then ran for the stairs. But just as I got there, I heard his door open. Turning back, I hoped against hope he'd changed his mind.

But no. I never saw him again. I only heard him, speaking from beyond the door. "You're a cold, airless void. You suck the air from my lungs. Why the hell can't you just breathe? Then maybe I could, too."

Anger flooded me again. I didn't come to talk about me. He had no *right* to talk about me! "What about Karl?" I demanded.

"Karl doesn't need me," he insisted.

"Then what does he need?"

"Breathe, damn it!"

"What the hell does that mean?" I was screaming, metaphorically bashing my brains out on a concrete wall. "What the *hell* does that mean?"

"Breathe!"

"I can't. It hurts!"

"Of course it does. Let it."

The door slammed, and I stood shivering in the dim hall.

IV

I couldn't return to work that day and spent a miserable night not sleeping, not knowing how I was going to tell Karl, not knowing why I even cared. I hadn't asked for this abuse. Probably I should just cut my losses and move on.

I dragged myself into the office the next morning, later than usual. I plopped down at my desk and stared at the papers, books, and sticky notes littering my workspace. I thought long but not too hard about throwing everything out, quitting my job, and moving a thousand miles away. Fantasized about all that, more like. It wasn't really thought, since thought requires logic and the only logic making its presence felt that morning was that I couldn't afford to start over, not financially, not emotionally.

I didn't notice Kaycee by my side until she cleared her throat and said, tentatively, "Jess?" She looked ashen, and her hands were trembling as they shuffled a piece of paper back and forth.

"Now what?" I wasn't at my most sympathetic just then. Or ever, I realized. How had I become so unfeeling?

"Harvey Jennings." She mouthed other words that didn't form, then shoved the paper at me.

I took it and read. Under a junior reporter's byline, a brief story described the finding of a body outside the apartments I had visited the other day. Harvey Jennings, age seventy-three, had apparently fallen from the roof to his death. Police were calling it a suicide, since he had no business being on the roof and no evidence of foul play had been uncovered. An investigation was ongoing.

I dropped the paper on my desk and stared at it. "Oh God, Kaycee. I killed him."

She looked right through me, not comprehending, and I knew I couldn't explain even if I had three lifetimes. So I didn't try. Kaycee eventually picked up the paper and wandered away, mumbling words I couldn't hear.

Karl heard the news on the radio that morning on his way to work. He called just before lunchtime and asked if we could get together. We met at a deli halfway between our respective offices, got a couple of reubens, and took a small table by the window.

"Did you meet him?" he asked.

I didn't quite know. Could our encounter be called a meeting? "Sort of."

"What did he say? Did he say anything about me?"

I looked into Karl's eyes, probably for the first time since I'd met him, and saw desperation. His one hope was gone, except whatever shards of it I now carried within me. What should I say? What *could* I say? Really, there was only one thing.

"Yes," I told him. "You were all he talked about."

I hadn't lied. Not exactly. A lot can be conveyed in a single word, if you know what it means and how to say it. Harvey's meaning unfolded in my heart and mind over the course of many months. I may be a slow student, but in the end I got it.

You probably think you know how the story ended. You think—no, you *want* it to be like this: Karl and I fell madly in love, destroyed both of our beds, got married, went through several more mattresses, and lived happily ever after. But no. It wasn't anywhere near that shallow.

We became good friends, almost brother and sister, and spent a lot of time repairing each other's brains. He told me how he and Martina fell apart, or at least as much as he knew, and I didn't for one nanosecond think about writing up and publishing his story. In return, I told him of my own sordid, unhappy flings. We picked up each other's tattered remains, stitched and glued them back together, restuffed the stuffing, and started down the road again like twin *Wizard of Oz* scarecrows. There's too much to tell, too much joy and pain to relate in a small space, but the one thing I learned through it all is this: you don't get the joy without the pain. So you might as well embrace them both. Inhale. Exhale. Breathe.

And Harvey Jennings . . . what was he? I doubt even he knew, but call him a sponge, soaking up other people's spills, drinking it all in until saturated. Maybe he had no choice but to wring himself dry. In so doing, he taught me that empathy is a gift, and for that I'll always be grateful. I draw some comfort in thinking he died to give me that gift, but every night as the darkness closes in, I fear he simply had too much of it for too long. Either way, wherever he is, I hope he's found some peace.

The Old Place

Leaves crunched beneath Samantha's feet as she pulled grandfather across autumn-dim grass toward the farmhouse where, Grandpa said, he'd grown up, raised his children, and lived until Grandma died and he couldn't stay anymore.

With each step she kicked a storm of leaves for the cool wind to whisk away.

A great oak overspread the lawn and cloaked the farmhouse in mystery. Samantha liked mystery. It broke her out in tingling goosebumps.

"You never knew Grandma," Grandpa said in his reedy voice. "She died before you were born."

"Is she in heaven now?" Samantha's wondering eyes lifted to the cloud of yellowing leaves.

Grandpa looked, too. "If heaven looks like that."

"It must!"

"That's her headstone, you see."

"Is she in the tree, Grandpa? Is the tree her?"

Grandpa patted Samantha's head and clumped up the steps onto the porch. His hand touched the old door, stroked it for a moment, then pulled.

Samantha's nose wrinkled at the ancient smells from within. Grandpa tugged her hand and they entered.

For a moment all was dark, then light grew and old smells gave way to aromas of turkey and stuffing and sweet potatoes and fresh baked pumpkin pie. Samantha heard a cry of joy as old as the world, and Grandpa nudged her forward into a pair of pale, shimmering arms that surrounded her and filled her with the warmth of their love.

"Oh my child!" Grandma said, tears in her eyes. "Now I truly am in heaven!"

Thank you for reading! Please leave a short, honest review wherever you purchased this book. I greatly appreciate it, and it will help others discover my books.

About the Author

Dale E. Lehman is an award-winning writer, veteran software developer, amateur astronomer, and bonsai artist in training. He principally writes mysteries, science fiction, and humor. In addition to his novels, his writing has appeared in *Sky & Telescope* and on Medium.com. He owns and operates the imprint Red Tales. He and his late wife Kathleen have five children, six grandchildren, and two feisty cats. At any given time, Dale is at work on several novels and short stories.

Visit https://www.DaleELehman.com to find out more about Dale's books.